The
Illustration
of Tommy T.
& Other Short Stories

The Illustration of Tommy T.

& Other Short Stories

G. J. Cook

**The New
Atlantian Library**

THE NEW ATLANTIAN LIBRARY
is an imprint of
ABSOLUTELY AMAZING eBOOKS
Published by Whiz Bang LLC, 926 Truman Avenue, Key West,
Florida 33040, USA.

For information contact:
Publisher@AbsolutelyAmazingEbooks.com

ISBN-13: 978-0692447161 (New Atlantian Library, The)
ISBN-10: 0692447164

The
Illustration
of Tommy T.
& Other Short Stories

TABLE OF CONTENTS

"He said, 'The china on the shelf is very fair to view
Wherefore should not mine outer self not correspond thereto?'

So forth he sailed to Borneo, a land that culture lacks
And there his money did bestow to purchase pricks and hacks

Now, never more to Chelsea might the luckless boy return
He knew himself too dreadful, quite; a thing his friends would spurn

And so he dwells in Borneo, a land that culture lacks
And there they all admire him so . . . they bring him heads in sacks."

- Andrew Lang

THE ILLUSTRATION OF

TOMMY T.

Tommaso Tataglia slowly turned in his high-back, leather-upholstered swivel chair and gazed into the large, well-lit, bust-view, three-sided mirror on the dressing table in front of him. His thick black hair fell loosely down over his parrot-green and gold Japanese kimono. The kimono was opened at the neck, and then closed to a "V" at his waist. It was held together with a bright, golden, silk sash. He undid the sash and slowly pulled open the gown. He opened the silver cigarette case, took out a cigarette, lit it, inhaled deeply, and placed the cigarette in the teeth of the silver dragon ashtray on the table. He had just finished applying the scented oil to his body and was examining the results. Through the two side mirrors he could see the twin black panthers slinking down both sides of his cheeks. Their eyes glowed red with the fervor of the hunt. Their keen claws extended and almost – but not quite – touched the brilliantly colored peacock which, displaying its handsome indigo and vermilion fan, covered the entire area from his lower lip to the cleft of his chin. He saw the two tiny suns geometrically placed on each of his cheekbones; their bright rays bursting forth in deep reds and yellows. In the center mirror he saw the twin, miniature asps which gracefully slithered across his upper lip; their tiny heads curled, poised and facing each other just under the bridge of his nose, while their tails coiled up at each end of his upper lip, resembling the twisted ends of a handlebar moustache. Sitting peacefully on each eyebrow, facing each other and pointing to the "All-Seeing-Eye" in the center of his forehead were two golden-brown spider monkeys. Their long tails hung down, curling into graceful circles at his temples. His thick, dark hair almost completely covered the small Sanskrit characters that ran across the very top of his forehead. The rest of his face was adorned with tiny shooting stars, comets with long, brightly colored tails trailing behind them, and minuscule quarter-moons. All were perfectly symmetrical in both design and color.

"Perfect." He said in a whisper – a thing he could not help saying each time that he looked at himself in a mirror. "Perfect."

He picked up the cigarette, inhaled deeply, allowing the thick, leadened smoke to run out of his nostrils, and set the cigarette down again. As he sat, reflectively staring at the silver dragon ashtray, he began to think. He thought of his first experience with skin illustration. He would never forget his first 'piece' . . .

I

THE SEDUCTION

TOMMY HAD JUST turned fourteen. The guys in the neighborhood had built a little clubhouse from scrap wood and cardboard. It stood in the center of a vacant lot over on one of the back streets. A few of them had secretly met there one night to get "Tattooed" – a word that, after having read Bradbury's, *The illustrated Man*, Tommy T. *(the name that he was known by in the neighborhood)* had ceased to use. 'Skin Illustration' was a much more descriptive term," he thought. "More artistic . . . More *magical.*"

≈ ≈ ≈

One of the guys had brought a bottle of *Higgins* India ink, some sewing needles and a bit of thread. He had taken the needles, placed them together, and then wrapped the thread tightly around the tips so that many punctures could be made with just one prick of the skin.

"My cousin Anthony showed me how to do it," the boy had said. "He got a lot of 'em."

They all took off their shirts, bared their forearms and commenced to have their initials etched into them.

It had hurt Tommy a little – and made him sweat too – but not as much as he had thought it would. When it was finished, all wiped, and the excess ink and blood cleaned away, he looked down at it. *"How small,"* he thought. *"And yet how good-looking it was. How 'handsome'."* It said: "Tommy T.," and had a miniature scroll drawn beneath it.

It *was* small. It could've been almost completely covered over with a poker chip . . . But that was the start of it.

TOMMY T. FINALLY had gotten his first tattoo – something that he had secretly wanted to do for a long time. He had also received a beating from his mother for "marking up his perfect body" – something which he knew was going to happen as soon as she noticed that it wouldn't come off with soap and water. And now it was all over and everything was all right, and he was satisfied . . . Satisfied, that is, until the scab of the tattoo had fallen off and the area around it had completely healed. It was about that time that Tommy T. began to experience a certain *vague* sensation of discontent; a sensation that would accompany him for many years to come. He would sit and look at his arm and think, *"Yes, the 'piece' was nice; yes, he liked it and all that . . . But." "But,"* he would then think again to himself, *"Wouldn't another one on my other forearm make my body look even better? More even?"* "Just a small one," he'd say. "Yeah, just a small one."

It was then that Tommy began taking the bus and traveling downtown by himself. Traveling down to the "sleazy" part of downtown. He had heard from someone that there were some 'Tattoo joints' on Market Street, down by the pawnshops and cheap bars, and so it was there that he wandered. It took him a few trips into that area to find it . . . But, in the end, he found what he was seeking. There was a certain barbershop where, when men left, they, not only dusted off their heads and shoulders, but some of them also rolled down their shirt-sleeves; rolled down their sleeves, apparently to cover up a piece of paper napkin that had been stuck to their forearms with Scotch tape – the same kind of procedure that the kid in the clubhouse had done to him when he finished his tattoo.

After a few days of staring at the place from across the street, Tommy mustered up enough courage to walk over and look directly into the window of the shop. The shop was typical – two chairs and some seats along the wall which were scattered with magazines. Typical – with the exception of one thing. In one corner of the shop was a small area that was surrounded by a low, wooden fence. The fence was about three feet high. Inside the fenced-in area sat an old man with unkempt, thinning grey hair. Down on the bridge of his nose rested a pair of thick-lensed, steel-rimmed glasses. He was wearing a yellowishy stained, strap T-shirt. His hairy, sagging arms and his chest were completely covered with strange, faded and blurry, blue markings. "Flash" posters, displaying a vast profusion of hearts, skulls, roses, snakes, daggers and the such, hovered on the walls behind the old man. As Tommy stared at that corner through the dirty glass in front of the barbershop he felt his stomach tighten a little. He wanted very badly to go in and see what it was all about. This *"Tattoo Joint"* thing that he had heard about. But, when the old man in the corner slowly looked up at him, Tommy's forehead broke into a cold sweat and he immediately turned and walked away.

≈ ≈ ≈

A few days later Tommy found the strength to enter the shop. He walked in and looked over at the corner. The old man that he had seen sitting in the 'pen' – *the traditional name for the work area used by Tattoo Artists of that era* – a few days before was not there. A bit confused as to what to do next, he walked over and sat in one of the chairs against the wall. When one of the barbers said, "You're next, son," he stuttered, "I . . . I . . . I'm waitin' for the guy in the corner." The barber looked at him for a moment, smiled and then shouted towards the back room. "Hey, Dutch! Ya got a customer!"

Dutch charged Tommy 50¢, tattooed a small monkey holding a red ball, onto his left forearm, and told him not to come back again until he was eighteen.

THE YEARS WENT by and Tommaso Tataglia collected more and more 'illustrations'. He sought out different Tattooists; lying about his age, if he had to, in order to get them to work on him. Tattoo Artists really aren't the kind of people who insist on ID . . . It was Tommy's cash that they insisted on. And *that* he always had.

The more work that he had done on him, the more trouble he began having finding just the 'right piece' to add to his 'collection' . . . And also the right place to put it. Every piece on him had to be – to his eyes, anyway – "Perfect".

As time passed, Tommy's thoughts centered more and more on *skin illustration*. It soon became apparent to his friends and family that everything Tommy looked at – a cloud in the sky, a picture in a magazine, even a plate of eggs . . . *Everything* his eye saw, his mind grasped as an illustration; a *representation,* that might be etched on either him, or someone else, in order to enhance one's being . . . one's *essence* . . . Even one's very *soul.* You could safely say that Tommy T. ate, drank and slept *Tattoo*.

Tommy was also beginning to have trouble getting dates with 'regular girls'. The girl that he had dated since he was thirteen had broken up with him; saying that her family would no longer allow her to see him because – as her father said – of all that "*shit that he was putting on himself.*" The only girls that wanted to date him were the ones that no one else wanted to date. And all they wanted to do was look at his illustrations.

About a year ago on a very hot day, Tommy had taken off his shirt in the kitchen to wash himself in the sink. His mother walked in, looked at his body, began crying, and left the room. He never again removed his shirt in the house after that unless he was in his own room.

His friends were also beginning to annoy him. Now, every time he would come around the corner, instead of saying: "Hey Tommy. What's up, man?" They would say something like: "Hey, here comes Tommy Tattoo!" Or: "Hey, Tommy! C'mon, man. Let's see all your pictures, man."

Tommy finally stopped going around the corner and dating girls . . . But he didn't stop getting illustrated. He began to spend more and more time by himself. He would spend hours in the library reading books on the history of tribal tattooing and skin illustration; and drawing fascinating designs that he imagined, in time, he would have etched onto his body. He also spent many hours in his room, gazing at his opulently adorned body in front of the dresser mirror.

On Tommy's seventeenth birthday, when asked what he wanted for a present, he requested a full sized, three-way mirror for his room. His parents just looked at him, shook their heads . . . and bought him one.

≈ ≈ ≈

Two or three times a week, Tommy would take the bus downtown and spend the day hanging around Dutch's Tattoo Parlor. He would sit around, smoke cigarettes, sip cheap whiskey with Dutch and listen to him – once again – tell how he first got started in 'the business'.

"I was a pretty good artist in my day, kid. Started out my career makin' designs on wallpaper," Dutch would say, after the whiskey had loosened his tongue up a bit. "Then I got into this business here. Makin' designs on people. Money wasn't as good, but I liked it. Opened my first shop right on the corner of Bowery an' Canal Street in New York City; just at the beginning of the war. Used to tattoo any serviceman in uniform for only 50¢. No matter what size tattoo he wanted. Just 50¢ for servicemen. Patriotic, ya' know."

"Did pretty good in them days, kid," he'd say, with a wistful look. "But then my eyes started goin' bad an' . . . " And then he would trail off; staring out the window of the shop, into the street.

Dutch showed Tommy how he mixed the powdered dye with Listerine to "ward off infection". He showed him which needles were used for outlining and which were used for shading. He showed him how he operated the "hammers" – the heavy, electric tattoo machines – by the use of a foot-peddle on the floor. Dutch showed him how to adjust the speed, or "flame", of the machines by regulating the dial on the power transformer that sat on the table. Once in awhile Dutch would even let Tommy help him while he was putting a piece on a customer.

"Here, kid, shave this guy's arm," he'd say. Or, "C'mere, kid, stretch this guy's skin so's I can get this goddamn ink in there."

ONE NIGHT, JUST after his eighteenth birthday, while lying in bed thumbing through some Tattoo books, absently massaging his last piece, and feeling that vague sensation of discontent, Tommaso Tataglia came to a decision. His uncle, who was a merchant seaman, had suggested that he go to sea. "Ya gotta do something with yourself, kid," he said. "Ya just can't sit around gettin' tattooed for the rest of your life. Livin' on the open sea is a great life, kid. You'll travel around the world for free and see all the seven wonders." His uncle even said that he would help him to get his seaman's papers.

Tommy *had* been thinking of traveling . . . But not to see the Seven Wonders of the World. He had been thinking of traveling to Japan. He had purchased some books on the art of Japanese *Irezumi*, and had been studying them in his room at night. An *Irezumi*, [Tattoo], according to one of the books, was a 'manifestation of a one's *inner self*. A protective cover . . . A defense . . . A *shield* against evil. It says: *Don't come too close to me. If you do, beware!*'

The books contained full-page photos of Japanese men and women that had gotten full-body Irezumi. One book said that these people were very secretive about displaying their bodies; and that many were members of small, exclusive *Nakamas* or, 'societies', where only members could view each other's Irezumi. Many of the people in the books also said that they felt that they had not merely *gotten* an Irezumi . . . But, that they had actually *become* Irezumi. And that was what Tommaso Tataglia wanted most in the whole world: To *become* Irezumi.

About six months ago he had come into an inheritance. A distant relative had passed away and left his family a large sum of money . . . A *very* large sum of money. He would use his share, he thought, to pay for his Irezumi.

That night, as he lie in bed thumbing through the books, he made up his mind. He would go to sea and travel to Japan. He didn't know, right at this moment, just exactly how he was going to accomplish it, but he was going to go to Japan, find one of those secret societies, become a member and have his entire body illustrated.

II

THE QUEST

WITH THE HELP of his uncle, Tommaso Tataglia finally got his seaman's papers and, at twenty years old, was working his way across the ocean as a stoker on a tramp steamer. The voyage was tedious and colorless. He also suffered from sea-sickness. During the trip Tommy spent most of his free time either walking alone on deck, or in his bunk reading Tattoo books.

Finally, after two months at sea, and making stops in Algiers, Hong Kong, and other smaller ports, Tommy's ship arrived in Sagami harbor . . . A small seaport, about fifty miles from Tokyo. The day after the ship arrived in port, Tommy packed his seaman's bag, collected his pay, walked down the ship's gangway and never returned.

It took him some time to find what he had come here for. Besides the language barrier, these *Irezumi* – like the books he read back home had stated – were very secretive people. At first he just, more-or-less, wandered the streets, talking with owners of food stands, or approaching shop owners. He would roll up his shirt-sleeves, showing his tattooed arms and ask, in pidgin-English: "Where Irezumi. Where Irezumi." The busy Japanese would just stare at him for a moment, and then turn away; either with a look of bewilderment, or mild disgust.

≈ ≈ ≈

One night, while sitting in one of the waterfront *Ginza* bars that dotted the harbor, he noticed two sailors, sitting

11

in a booth near the rear of the bar. They were both drunk. One had rolled up his sleeve and was showing a full, arms-length tattoo of a bright green dragon to his companion. "Yeah," he was saying as he waved his arm in front of his friend, "I got it last night from one of these 'Chink' tattoo artists. Hurt like a bitch. Cost me a month's pay. Waddaya think?" The other sailor just sat there nodding his head up and down saying, "Um-m-m-m-m."

"Waddaya mean, 'Um-m-m-m-m'," the tattooed sailor slurred. "You're too goddamn drunk to apre . . . apre . . . see anything anyway!" and began rolling down his sleeve.

When Tommy saw the sailor's arm he quickly got up, approached the booth and said with a smile, "Hey, mate. Let's see what ya got there." The sailor turned and eyed him warily. Before he had the chance to say something nasty like, "Fuck off, asshole!", Tommy unbuttoned his shirt and displayed his arms and chest.

The sailor stared at Tommy's work for a whole minute and then finally said: "Mate, that sure is some nice work ya got there. Where'd ya get it?"

"In the States," Tommy replied. "Where'd ya get yours?"

"This little dragon here, ya mean?" he said as he gently stroked the beast's brilliant, gold and emerald colored scales which covered most of his right arm and shoulder. "Well, I got this here little serpent from a Chink Tattoo Artist about five blocks from here."

"Will you take me there?" Tommy said, trying to appear calm and composed. As he spoke, he could feel his stomach beginning to tighten. "Take me there, mate and I'll give you ten bucks."

"You'll give me twenty," the sailor said.

"Deal," said Tommy. "Let's go."

≈ ≈ ≈

After a long period of having to almost drag him away from the bar, Tommy and the sailor left and headed to the place to where the sailor had said that he had gotten his Tattoo.

"Here it is, mate," the sailor said when finally they reached a small wooden, two-story building that was, in actuality, almost a half mile from the bar. "It's up there," he said, pointing to the second floor of the building. "Now gimme the twenty."

Tommy turned his back, opened his wallet, pulled out a twenty and handed it to the sailor.

"Thanks," said the sailor, walking away. "An' good luck to ya, mate."

Tommy watched as the drunken sailor wove his way down the street and out of sight. Then he turned and looked up at the building. It was sandwiched in by similar structures which lined both sides of the street. This particular house appeared to be a somewhat shoddy structure. The wooden panels on the sides of the small house were unpainted and warping. He looked up at the rice-paper windows on the second floor. There were no lights. The place seemed deserted. *"It's late,"* he thought. *"Maybe everyone's asleep."*

"Hallo!" he said at first, a bit loudly. He was determined, this time, to find what he had come all the way across the sea seeking. When no one answered, he said in faltering Japanese, *"Konnichi wa! Konnichi wa!"* But still no one answered. He was just about to leave, thinking to himself that he would have to come all the way back here tomorrow, when, above him, a window panel slid open and someone stuck out their head. The silhouetted figure looked down at him for a moment and then said something to him in Japanese that he did not understand.

"*Irezumi,*" said Tommy, looking up at the blank face. "I want *Irezumi.*"

"*Saru!*" said a man's voice. "Go away! No Irezumi here. No Tattoo!"

Tommy was not going to be put off so easily. If this person didn't actually *give* tattoos, then he knew who did; and if he had to stay here all night until he found out, then that's just what he was going to do.

"*Irezumi!*" he shouted this time. "*Irezumi . . . Please!*"

For a moment there was silence. Tommy waited, staring up at the pitch-black head hovering above him.

Then, in English, the voice said, "Too late, now. Come back tomorrow night. Six O'clock," and slid the window back with a sharp click.

BACK IN HIS small room Tommy relaxed on his bed listening to the fog horns moaning at the mouth of the harbor. While watching the smoke from his cigarette slowly curling up to the ceiling, he thought about the next day. He was wondering about how much it was going to cost him to get this 'thing' that he desired so badly, done. He had brought the entire share of his inheritance with him; not spending even one penny of it. "I hope it's enough," he said to himself as he lay on his back, blowing smoke up at the ceiling.

He was also wondering if this *Hori* [*engraver* or *carver;* the Japanese slang for *Tattoo Artist*] would even agree to do it. The book said that hardly anyone 'white' would have the desire – or the courage – to have their whole body illustrated. He had read that, to get a whole "body piece" took years . . . And, also cost a small fortune. "I hope it's enough," he said to himself again, as he drifted into sleep. "I hope it's enough."

≈ ≈ ≈

The next evening at four o'clock Tommy took a long, hot shower, shaved and put on some clean clothes. He went down into the street and bought some food from a street vender. Tommy pointed to what he wanted and held out a handful of Japanese coins to the man. The man took out a few coins and handed Tommy his order: Three pieces of smoked fish, draped across a clump of sticky, white rice – served in an open cardboard container, complete with a small set of chopsticks and napkin. While standing there eating, he could feel his stomach. It was getting tighter and tighter.

He ate quickly – wolfing down the fish and rice – and then sat around impatiently, chain-smoking, until he figured that it was time to start walking over to the place where he was to meet the man that had spoken to him the night before.

The walk seemed to take forever, but, finally, after a few turns down wrong alleys, he arrived at the house. In the setting sun it looked even more rundown than it had appeared to him the night before.

"*Konnichi wa.*" Tommy called, looking up at the window. There was no answer. He called again; and then a few times more, but still, there was no answer. A strong sensation of disappointment and frustration flooded over him. "Sonofabitch!" he said, under his breath, as he turned and began to walk away; feeling that he had been "blown off" once again. As he stopped to light a cigarette, he noticed a small man on the other side of the street walking in his direction. The man was completely dressed in black. He wore long pants, a long-sleeved, collarless jacket that was fastened all the way to his neck, and a black, silk, *beanie-type* cap on his head. The cap was too large for the man's head and was pulled down very low over his forehead; which seemed, to Tommy, a bit *odd*. It was pulled down so far that it completely covered his eyebrows. As the strange looking man drew closer, he stepped off the curb and began crossing the damp, cobblestone street. His high, platformed, wooden sandals made a sharp, clopping sound as he crossed. When he reached the other side, he stepped up on the curb and approached Tommy as if he were going to say something . . . But then just continued walking right past. Tommy stared at the man as he walked by. As he passed, Tommy looked down and thought that he saw a strange red design tattooed on the back of the man's left hand. It appeared to be a small, crimson flame with some kind of oriental character placed in its center. When the man approached the building where Tommy was to meet the Hori, he stopped, fished in his pocket, pulled out a set of keys and began unlocking the door. While the man was turning the key in the lock Tommy noticed an identical flame and inscription on the man's right hand. The man stood motionless in the opened doorway for a moment and then, slowly turned, stared at Tommy and said, in a quiet voice: "Come."

TOMMY FOLLOWED THE small man up a narrow, winding staircase. When they reached the second floor the man slipped off his wooden sandals, pointed to Tommy's boots and said, "Take off boots."

Tommy undid his heavy boots, pulled them off and stood looking around the room in his stocking feet. It was a loft type dwelling; somewhat small and sparse of furniture – a typical Japanese abode. Parts of the apartment were sectioned off by screens containing opaque, rice-paper windows. The man led Tommy to a small partitioned, studio-like area in the rear of the apartment, pointed to some pillows that surrounded a large *tatami* mat, situated in the middle of the room and said, "Sit, please." Then he left the room.

Tommy removed his seaman's jacket, hung it on a wooden peg on the wall and sat down on one of the pillows. The area that he was in was nearly bare except for two lamp tables, the mat, four pillows and two enormous wooden chests. The chests appeared to be made of hand carved teakwood and were adorned with bright brass hinges and handles. They were highly polished. The floors, walls and ceiling were made of a blond wood which Tommy could not identify. They were also highly polished. Although the apartment was not large, the modest amount of furniture, and discreet placement of what there was, gave the place a feeling of lofty expanse; while the small, square, lantern-type lighting fixtures positioned on the low tables, gave each area a soft, *homey* glow.

Tommy sat nervously on the pillow waiting for the man to return. He heard some shuffling and turned to see what it was. He could see the man's shadow moving around behind one of the screens He wondered what the man was doing.

"Can I smoke?" Tommy asked, looking at the moving shadow.

"Smoke." answered the shadow.

Tommy lit a cigarette, placed it in the teeth of a small, silver, dragon ashtray that sat on the mat, and waited.

At last he heard a soft padding behind him. He turned and there stood the Hori. He was wearing a black silk kimono that was exquisitely decorated with beautiful red and grey dragons. When he looked up at him he saw that the man's head had been shaved and was completely covered with hundreds of minute red and black tattoos of, what appeared to be, Japanese characters. At first glance, the design resembled a colorfully embroidered skull cap.

The man was holding a small, black-lacquered tray in his hands. Two small, thick, black porcelain cups and a black, long-necked, decanter sat on the tray. The cups and decanter were also decorated with dragons. Tommy could smell the sake as small whiffs of it steamed gently from the decanter.

The man sat down opposite Tommy, placed the tray between them, poured the sake, and handed one of the cups to Tommy. Then he reached into his kimono, removed a pack of cigarettes and lit one; letting the smoke drift lazily above his head.

He finally said, "My name is Mitsuaki Ohwada. I am called *Horikin* . . . The *'Carver of Gold'*. What can I do for you?"

"My name is Tommaso Tataglia," Tommy answered a bit shyly, " . . . my friends call me Tommy T. I came here from America. I . . . I want a Tattoo,"

Tommy then thought of how witlessly he had just answered the Hori's question. He wanted *much* more than just 'a *Tattoo*'.

The man stared at Tommy and said nothing. He took a long drag from his cigarette, letting the smoke slowly drift out of his nostrils and then said, in perfect English, "Who sent you to me?"

Tommy was a bit surprised by the man's seemingly effortless command of English. "A sailor," he said. "I met him in a bar last night. He had a dragon tattooed on his right arm."–Horikin nodded knowingly–"It was beautiful. I asked him where he had gotten it. He took me here. He said you were a 'dumb . . .'" Tommy stopped short of the sailor's full description – not wishing to offend Horikin.

Noticing Tommy's apparent discomfort, Horikin said, with a smile and a slight glint in his eye, "It is sometimes more advantageous for one of intelligence, when dealing with one of no intelligence, to be thought of as only a '*dumb chink*'."

Tommy smiled.

"*So*," Horikin went on. "You wish to be illustrated with such a dragon?"

"*Illustrated*," Tommy thought. "Yes," he said. "I want to be illustrated. But not just with a dragon. I . . . I . . . I want," he faltered, trying to explain to the Hori his exact desire, "I . . . I want a full-body Irezumi." He said at last. "I want to *become* Irezumi."

Horikin sat motionless for a long time. Then he said: "Do you have any . . . illustrations?"

"Yes," answered Tommy.

"May I see them?" said Horikin.

Tommy rose, removed his shirt and faced the Hori.

Horikin stared at Tommy's arms and torso for a long while; And then, placing his hand over his mouth to conceal a budding smile, he said, "Turn around . . . Please."

Tommy noticed Horikin smiling. With his face reddening from embarrassment and anger, he turned and exposed his back.

This time Horikin, no longer able to contain himself, broke into a peal of vigorous laughter.

Hurt and angered by the Hori's coarse response to, what he considered to be *"Perfect"* illustrations, Tommy wheeled, faced the sniggering man and blurted, "What the Fuck is so funny?"

"You look like a . . . *comic book*," said Horikin, smiling widely. "Those are not illustrations . . . They are *cartoons*.

Tommy was just about to lose his temper and say something he probably would regret later, when Horikin stood up, undid his kimono and let it fall to the floor.

"This . . . is illustration." he said as he turned slowly in front of Tommy, clad only in a white *Fundoshi* [loincloth]. *"This* . . . is *Irezumi*. Not that. *That,*" he said, still rotating; proudly displaying himself, *"That* is . . . *iketenai. Shit."*

Tommy gazed with absolute awe at Horikin's pivoting body. To see a photo of an Irezumi in a magazine was one thing . . . But to *see* an Irezumi in the flesh – so close-up – was like seeing a photo of a tornado, and then, *seeing* one first hand; reeling and lurching through the countryside.

The small man's body was alive with warring Gods and leering Demons. Around his arms and legs golden carp and deep blue catfish swam through black, foaming, waters, while green and grey dragons soared through lightening bolts that crashed and raged. Across Horikin's entire back, with his terrifying face, and on a throne of flames, sat *Fudo,* the *"Immobile One"*. In his right hand, a sword to slay demons; in his left, a lasso to bind them with.

Tommy stared at Horikin's Irezumi . . . Completely overwhelmed by the sight – the absolute *realness* – of it.

≈ ≈ ≈

Finally, after revealing his Irezumi to Tommy – as a sorcerer or magician might reveal some 'divine enigma' to a young apprentice – Horikin calmly bent down, picked up his kimono, slipped it on and sat back down on his pillow. Tommy, overwhelmed, still stood.

"Please sit," said the Hori.

Tommy hesitated for a moment, staring into space – *as though he were witnessing a divinely spiritual illusion slowly fading into nothingness* – and then sat down.

"Tommaso Tataglia," said Horikin, " . . . may I call you Tommy-san?"

"Yes," answered Tommy.

"Tommy-san," continued Horikin, "You want, as you say, to '*become* Irezumi'".

"Yes," said Tommy. "Yes . . . Very much. Can you do it for me?"

"*Can* I do it?" Horikin said, with a faint smile. "Yes I *can* do it. But are you sure that this is what you want?

21

Really sure? There is an old adage, Tommy-san," he continued. "It says: 'It is one thing to *beckon* the Gods . . .But it is quite another if they actually *appear* before you'."

Tommy stared at Horikin. He was having trouble comprehending the man's meaning. Finally he said, "I know what I want. Will you do it? I have some money. I can pay."

"*Can* you pay?" said Horikin, now smiling like a Cheshire cat. "Do you *really* know the price for *becoming* Irezumi?"

"The price?" asked Tommy; still a bit confused. "What do you mean? I *said* that I have money."

Horikin stood up abruptly, adjusted his kimono and, walking toward the stairs, said: "Come back in one week. In that time I want you to think hard about the price of becoming Irezumi. Think very hard. If, after that, you still wish to be illustrated by me, come back and we will talk."

Tommy, still puzzled about what Horikin had said, and the abrupt manner in which he was now acting, just shook his head and rose to his feet, while slowly buttoning his shirt. He walked over to his boots and was about to pull them on when Horikin said: "Before you leave, please take off all of your clothes. I wish to look at your body."

Tommy – now more than a little perplexed – stared at Horikin for a moment; and then, a bit reluctantly, removed his shirt, pants, underwear and socks, and stood naked in the middle of the room.

While Tommy was undressing, Horikin walked over and opened one of the large teakwood chests. He reached in and took out a large sketch pad, a small bottle of ink and some fine-tipped pens and pencils. He then sat down on the mat and said: "Tommy-san. Please come here and stand in front of me." Tommy did so. Then, after quickly sketching something on the pad, he said, "Turn around . . . Slowly, please." Tommy turned around in a slow circle while Horikin rapidly sketched, turned over a leaf, and then, sketched some more.

Finally Horikin put down the pad, rose to his feet and said: "Thank you. Please get dressed now." As he walked to the stairs he said, without turning to Tommy: "Think about it. If your decision is yes, come back in one week. Six in the evening. If not, nice to have met you, sir. Good night." Horikin then turned and disappeared behind one of the screens.

≈ ≈ ≈

Tommy spent the next seven days in virtual torment. He had heard what the Hori had said to him, but couldn't quite figure out exactly what he meant by "the price". Was he talking about money? Was he talking about the vast amount of time it was going to take to have his body illustrated? What, *exactly,* did he mean? "What's the difference, anyway," Tommy finally declared impatiently. "I *want* to be illustrated; I'm *going* to be illustrated; and *that* is that. If not by him, than by someone else. And *Fuck* "the price". I didn't come all the way over here to talk riddles. I came here to get illustrated!"

ON THE SEVENTH day, precisely at 6 PM, Tommaso Tataglia arrived in front of Horikin's building. He was about to call up when, above him, the window slid open. Horikin stuck out his head and smiled. "Come up," he said. "The door is unlocked."

Tommy ascended the winding staircase. When he reached the top he undid his laces, slipped off his boots, and stood, waiting for Horikin to greet him.

"Come in, Tommy-san," said Horikin's voice from behind one of the screens. "I'm in the studio."

Tommy entered the small area where he and Horikin had first met seven days ago. Horikin was sitting on the tatami mat, clothed only in his white *fundoshi*. As he moved, perspiration caused his Irezumi to gleam and shimmer.

He was surrounded by colored ink-drawings and black-and-white sketches of various animals, birds and other curious, mythical creatures – both human and beast.

"Sit," said Horikin, gesturing to the mat without looking up. "Drink." he continued, pointing to the tray that held the bottle of sake and cups.

Tommy sat, poured a cup of sake and sipped the steaming liquid while staring intently at the exquisite drawings lying on the mat. They were absolutely stunning. Matchless in design and color. Tommy had never seen anything like them before. Not even in the magazines that he had read. He was just about to ask the Hori where he had obtained these works of art when Horikin spoke: "I have created these illustrations myself," he said, looking over at Tommy as if he had just read his mind. "They are for you . . . That is, if you have sincerely contemplated what we discussed. And, after pondering, you still have decided to . . . become Irezumi." he said, with a retiring smile.

For a moment Tommy thought that the Hori was making fun of him again, but dismissed it. And then, in a rather *urbane* tone he said: "Yes, I have thought about what you told me. About the price that I would have to pay to become Irezumi, and have come to a decision. I will pay the price." Tommy stared at Horikin hoping that he had convinced him by speaking in such an *elegant* manner.

Horikin said nothing. Finally, he looked up from his drawings and stared ardently at Tommy for a long while without speaking. Then he smiled broadly and said, in a somewhat intimate tone, "Tommy-san . . . You are full of shit. *(Tommy noticed for the first time that both of Horikin's incisor teeth were capped in solid gold.)* You are full of shit when you say that you have truly contemplated the price to be paid for having your entire body illustrated." He reached over, poured himself a cup of sake, sipped, and then he went on. "I knew when I first spoke with you a week ago, that your mind was already made up. I knew that there was nothing that was going to keep you from fulfilling your desire . . . Your *obsession.* No price was going to hold you back from becoming Irezumi. I do not admire your reckless naivety . . . But I *do* admire your courage and determination." The Hori took another sip and continued. "I have decided to be your *shokunin* . . . your artisan. I will do my best to turn your body into a thing of beauty and power. All of my vitality has gone into the creation of these figures that I have sketched here," he said, pointing to the sheets of drawings and sketches strewn around him, " . . . and, when you have become fully illustrated, their magnificence – along with their potency – will be transferred into your body. Your body will, in time, be transformed into a . . . *shinden* (he hesitated, as if trying to find the right translation to express his feelings) .

. . *a temple,* in which your *honshitsu . . . essence,* will forever dwell while you are alive.

Horikin hesitated, and then stared directly into Tommy's eyes for a long time. "Tommy-san . . . The price that you will pay for this gift is this." Horikin hesitated again for a moment, and then went on. "You will be required to endure unendurable pain for days and weeks, and even years, on end. You will be forced to sleep in the most uncomfortable positions for months while your Irezumi heals. The pain at times will become so great that you will strongly consider giving up; leaving your Irezumi only partially completed. Out of every one hundred persons that come to me requesting full-body Irezumi, only one remains until his Irezumi is fully completed. Due to the extensive scarring over most of your body, your skin will not be able to perspire, or 'breath' properly. As a result, your life span will be shortened. You will live the remainder of your life without ever again being able to come into any *real* social contact with, so-called 'normal', people. You will no longer be able to venture out of doors unless your Irezumi is fully covered. No matter what the temperature, you will be compelled to be fully dressed. If people see your Irezumi, they will shun and humiliate you. You will never be able to hold an ordinary job. And, Tommy-san, if, in the future, you may require a major operation . . . Will you allow the surgeon to cut into you . . . To sever your Irezumi? . . . Your *Power?*"

Horikin stopped for a moment and then looked down at his illustrations. He lit a cigarette, inhaled deeply and then said: "These, and much, much more, are the *price* one pays . . . the price that one pays to the world for possessing such *ban-no* . . . Such *omnipotence.*" Horikin then looked back up at Tommy.

"How much am I going to have to pay you for this," Tommy said, staring back at Horikin.

Horikin slowly shook his head and smiled at Tommy's sheer determination. Then he became serious again. "My *'payment'* for providing you with this unique gift of beauty and power will be this." Horikin hesitated for a moment, took a long pull on his cigarette and then went on. "*I will* decide *what* illustration is put *where* on your body. You will have no say in it. You must trust my judgment completely." The Hori then began shuffling the sketches around; acting as if his were preoccupied with them.

"You will possess the Irezumi – and its power – for as long as you live. It will be your responsibility to care for it. You will be the 'guardian'–so to speak–of the temple." Horikin continued, in a soft, almost *detached* tone. "But, you must agree that, upon your death, your body, along with the Irezumi, is returned to me."

"To do *what* with," asked Tommy. He was beginning to become a bit confused.

"I can say no more," said Horikin, still staring at the drawings. "Do you agree?"

Tommy stared at Horikin's Irezumi. It glistened and danced before him.

"Yes," he said, without hesitation.

"Good!" said Horikin, stacking the drawings to one side of the mat. "Take off your shirt, Tommy-san. Let's begin."

III

The Illustration

Horikin did not use the electric machines traditionally employed in the West. He had them, and had used them on the drunken sailor – but just to get him out of his studio quickly. Horikin applied the traditional Eastern method of Tattooing on Tommy's body. He used various sized needles, spliced onto long bone, ivory or bamboo sticks, with black, silk thread. Neither were the inks the same as the ones purchased from catalogs by Western Tattooists. Each shade and color was created from scratch by Horikin's own hand. Using a mortar and pestle, blocks of uniquely rare pigments were crushed and pulverized into a fine talc. The different colored powders, along with rare vegetable dyes, were then matched and mixed together to produce the magnificent tones that would be used to illustrate Tommy's body. Some colors – blues, greys and reds especially – were mixed together with pulverized pearl talcum, or cadmium, in order to produce an "iridescent" effect on the skin. The talc was then mixed with a liquid that had been laced with cocaine. This was done in order to lessen the pain that would occur from the constant puncturing of the skin with needles.

Each section of Tommy's body that was to be worked on was first shaved free of any hair and then washed down with a natural disinfectant. His arms were the first to be illustrated. Horikin meticulously covered – or worked around – Tommy's old designs; cleverly transforming the

29

parts of the old piece that wouldn't cover well into swirls or flowers in the new illustration.

The sharp, black outline of the design was set into the skin first. This was then allowed to heal fully. Later came the brighter colors, to fill in the design. When they had healed, Horikin used the blues and greys for shading, and to bring out the design more distinctly.

≈ ≈ ≈

It took nine months for the Hori to fully illustrate Tommaso Tataglia's both arms – Sometimes working for hours on an intricate part of the design only two inches in diameter. Although Tommy suffered much pain and discomfort having his arms illustrated, he was still impatient. He asked Horikin to work on other parts of his body while his arms were healing. The Hori refused, saying that, to subject the body to such excessive shock, might cause his immune system to become overloaded and, consequently, shut down. This could possibly result in a fatal infection.

Tommy's legs – fronts first, then the backs – were next. Then came his chest and diaphragm – upper, then lower. Next the Hori began the laborious work of covering Tommy's entire back and buttocks. It was the most painful portion of the Irezumi for Tommy to endure. But that was only because Horikin had saved the hands, feet, neck, face, head . . . and penis . . . until last. The palms of his hands were tattooed with bright red and yellow flames and inscribed with sacred Hindu symbols. His feet were decorated with miniature sea-turtles: an Eastern symbol of good luck. Then Horikin shaved Tommy's entire face and head. He decorated Tommy's face with sacred animals and fortuitous stellar constellations. The same design that he wore on his own head he tattooed onto Tommy's. He told Tommy that the characters on his head were really Sanskrit, not Japanese; repeating, like a chant, the Hindu name of God hundreds of times. While he was creating the cap, the Hori told him the story of a blind Buddhist monk who was saved from being torn to pieces by demons by having his entire body covered with the sacred teachings of the Illustrious Buddha. "The only part of his body that had been forgotten were his ears," said Horikin, while working on Tommy's head. "When the demons entered the priest's house all they could see were his ears. So they ripped them off and took them away with them." Then he laughed and said with a smile, "Don't worry, Tommy-san. The demons won't get *your* ears." Horikin covered them both with sacred scriptures.

THE ILLUSTRATION OF Tommy T. took seven – long – years. In those seven years, just as the Hori had foretold, Tommaso Tataglia had suffered unendurably. He was compelled to sleep in the most awkward and uncomfortable positions – always taking care not to roll over in his sleep – so that his Irezumi would heal properly. For the first week after each section of his back was worked on, Tommy got almost no sleep at all. When Horikin tattooed Tommy's penis – always the last, and most painful part of the anatomy to be worked on – Tommy collapsed and spent the next four days in delirium and fever. There were moments when Tommy felt like giving up and – leaving his Irezumi unfinished – board a ship and return to the States. But he never did. Every time the pain became unbearable, Tommy thought of Horikin's Irezumi and how beautiful and 'perfect' it was. "I *will* become Irezumi," he would repeat over and over to himself, during these episodes, "I *will* become Irezumi!"

≈ ≈ ≈

Having no real home or friends in Sagami, Horikin invited Tommy to stay with him at his studio while he was creating Tommy's Irezumi. Tommy accepted; renting – *at Tommy's insistence* – a small, screened-off area of the loft to sleep in. Sometimes, at night, when the pain got too much, Tommy would groan pitifully. Horikin, hearing him, would come to lay cool, damp towels that had been soaked in healing herbs, onto his feverish body. He also prepared a special diet for Tommy. One that would keep his body trim, healthy and fit enough to fight off infections. To keep him busy while working on his Irezumi, Horikin allowed Tommy to assist him in small ways. He would send Tommy out – only at night, of course – to purchase the blocks of pigment. He also allowed him to 'prep' the "Western" customers.

It was during that time, while living with Horikin, that Tommy met some of the men and women in Horikin's *Nakama*. They were, as he had read, a very close-knit group. Shrouded in secrecy and mystique. Although the members of the Nakama were polite to Tommy, they never really engaged in any significant conversation with him. When Tommy asked Horikin if he would be allowed to join the Nakama when his Irezumi was completed, Horikin told him that he had already brought it up at a meeting. A vote had been taken and the members voted against his request.

"Why, Horikin?" Tommy asked.

"You are not Japanese," answered Horikin.

≈ ≈ ≈

There were also some evenings when all the members of the Nakama would meet in Horikin's studio. On these occasions Tommy was politely asked to leave the studio for a few hours. He wondered what they were doing while he was gone. He could hear their chattering from the open window as he walked down the street. They seemed to be celebrating or *toasting* to something. Exactly *what* they were doing was a mystery to him.

Tommy also had become aware that one of the large teakwood chests in Horikin's studio was never opened in his presence. When he asked why, the Hori would only say that the knowledge of the contents of that chest was reserved only for Nakama members. "But, someday perhaps you *will* come to know, Tommy-san," he would add, with a vague, inscrutable look on his face. "Perhaps someday you *will* be present when the chest is opened."

EIGHT YEARS AFTER Tommy had arrived in Sagami he began making preparations to return to the States. There was no real reason for him to remain in Japan any longer. His Irezumi was completed and had fully healed, he was homesick . . . And he was running low on money. He signed on board a freighter that was bound for San Francisco. It was due to leave in a week. Although he had never received any replies to previous letters written, Tommy wrote to his family stating his whereabouts, and that he would soon be back in the States. He packed his small belongings into his seaman's bag, placed it in the corner of his room and waited.

On the day of his departure, a few hours before his ship was to sail, Tommy said his goodbyes to Horikin.

Tommy walked into the studio where Horikin was working. "Sayonara Horikin," he said. "I'll write you when I arrive in the States."

Horikin sat, seemingly absorbed in pounding a small block of pigment into powder in the mortar. "You will find no peace there, Tommy-san," he said, after a long silence. "Neither will you find any here," he added, looking earnestly into the marble bowl, as if something very profound had just been discovered there. "Sayonara, Tommy-san. And remember to always keep our legal agreement on your person," he added, placing another small block of pigment into the mortar.

Tommy unconsciously felt in his jacket pocket to make sure that the document was still there. Of course, it was. He stood and stared at the Hori for a moment, then turned and slung his seaman's bag over his shoulder and walked toward the steps.

"Wait, Tommy-san," called Horikin.

Tommy turned and faced Horikin.

"Take this, Tommy-san." The Hori carefully handed Tommy the silver dragon ashtray. Tommy and Horikin's hands both held the ashtray for a moment. Then Horikin released his grip.

"Now, Go!" Horikin turned and began to pound the mortar, almost furiously, with the pestle.

Tommy slipped the ashtray into his jacket pocket,

turned, and walked down the stairs into the street.

Horikin could hear the dry thudding of Tommy's boots on the cobblestones outside.

"Goodbye, Tommy-san," he said.

IV
THE PRICE

O N THE VOYAGE home Tommaso Tataglia was all but ostracized by the rest of the crew. Even though he always wore his blue, long-sleeved work shirt completely buttoned at the neck and cuffs, the men found it difficult to carry on even a general conversation with him without becoming distracted by the bizarre appearance of his face. In the middle of discussing some problem with him at his work station, they would stop in mid-sentence, stare for a moment, and then point at his face and say something like: "Jesus, mate. Life is tough enough. What the hell did you go an' do *that* for." Tommy would just stare back at them for a moment without answering and then continue to discuss the problem. Some of the men even began calling him *'Queequeg'*, after the Tattooed harpooner in Melville's *Moby Dick*.

Tommy never responded to these insults and always performed his shipboard duties well. On his off hours he tried his best to keep completely to himself . . . To himself and his Irezumi, that is. Tommy could stand in front of a mirror and stare at it for hours. He would become entranced with the infinitesimally perfect detail of a lotus petal, or how the foam of a wave curved and broke in just the right place on his arm. "Perfect," he would say, after gazing into a mirror – sometimes for a full half an hour – at a one-inch-square section of his arm. *"Perfect."*

The Illustration of Tommy T.

AFTER TWO MONTHS at sea the ship finally docked at the harbor in San Francisco. Tommy collected his pay, gathered up his small belongings and came ashore. Horikin had been right. It soon became apparent to Tommy that there was literally nowhere he could venture – shopping, dining, or just out for a walk – where he wasn't gawked at, or annoyed, by someone. Some – especially young people – would point and say unpleasant, or offensive things. Others would approach him and request a photo of him – with either themselves or their children in it, of course. Tommy would, as politely as possible, decline and walk away.

The world outside of his Irezumi was becoming more and more distasteful to Tommaso Tataglia.

At a maritime clothiers Tommy purchased a full navel officer's dress uniform. Black trousers, white officer's cap and a full-length black top-coat. He also purchased a pair of black high-topped work boots, black leather gloves, a black crew-neck sweater and a pair of dark, aviator's glasses. This was what he wore every time he ventured out into the street. He would pull the brim of the cap far down over his forehead. His hair had grown back, but it did not hide his illustrated face. He wore the dark aviator's glasses too. But that did not help much either. People would still disturb and irritate him wherever he went.

≈ ≈ ≈

There came a time when Tommy no longer traveled about during the day. He would spend his days in the small room that he had rented above a waterfront bar; lying on his bed dozing, or reading and smoking cigarettes, until dark. It was only when the sun had fully set below the

38

horizon that Tommy would dress in his rather eccentric attire and venture out into the streets of San Francisco. He also began spending more and more time standing in front of a large dressing mirror that he purchased and had hung on the back of his room door. In his solitude, Tommaso Tataglia was becoming more and more engrossed . . . *lost* . . . in the infinite domain of his Irezumi.

AFTER SIX MONTHS wandering about the West Coast, Tommy T. decided it was time to make the three thousand mile journey home. He traveled by night, mostly. Hitching rides with truckers wired on Benzedrine, or on the back of some farmer's flat-bed pickup. Sometimes, after making a few dollars working an odd job, he would catch a midnight bus as far as the ticket would carry him.

He slept where he could. In a farmer's barn, in a hobo jungle, or sometimes, just by a running stream. He thought of the mysterious *Illustrated Man* in Bradbury's novel, and how he was becoming much like him. In a strange, melancholy way, it made him feel good.

Every so often Tommy would take out the silver dragon ashtray, hold it in his hand and think of Horikin . . . *"You will find no peace, Tommy-san."* He wondered how Horikin was doing. He had written him only once since he had arrived back in the States. He never received an answer. Tommy also wondered what Horikin wanted with his body after he died. Did he want to burn it, or something like that? Some kind of weird, *cult* thing that the Nakama perform? *"It didn't matter,"* he thought. He wouldn't be around to find out anyway.

TOMMY ARRIVED IN his hometown in the spring of the

year. It was a mistake to go there. The neighborhood – the picture of the one that he had stored in his mind, the one that he had cherished – was completely gone. The lot where the old clubhouse had been was now a two-story, brick townhouse. The sweetshop that used to be on the corner was now an auto parts store. He had stopped by to see Dutch on his way into town. The whole block where the barbershop/tattoo parlor once was had been torn down, and a modern shopping center was being constructed in its place. The only familiar structure still standing in the area was the one that housed *Grant's Bar and Grill* across the street. Tommy walked in and asked a bartender, who he did not recognize, about the tattoo parlor across the street and Dutch. The bartender didn't know what he was talking about.

Most of Tommy's friends had gotten married and moved away. The ones that did remain were either on welfare, or unemployment; and spent most of their days – and nights – in the few local bars that were left.

"*Tommy T.!*" they would shout, once they recognized him. "*Ya crazy sonofabitch! C'mere, man, an' let me buy ya a drink.*"

Then, when he would get close enough for them to realize that he wasn't wearing a beard, would come the predictable: "Oh, Christ, man. What the *Fuck* did you do to your face! Oh, *Christ,* Tommy. Look at ya!"

When he asked about his parents he was told that they had sold the house after his father had had a stroke, and had moved into a retirement community up in Maplewood. "Ya can't go an' see 'em like that, Tommy," they would say, pointing to his face. "It'll break your mother's heart an' probably kill your poor father."

Tommy got the address from one of the local store owners that had known him from when he was "just a kid" and went to see his parents. He waited until it was dark and then walked up to the small cottage that they were living in, and peered through one of the windows. His mother stood in the kitchen washing a glass. She looked up and, for a moment, Tommy thought that she had seen him. But she didn't, and went back to rinsing the glass. He walked around to the back of the house and, through the living room window, saw his father. He was sitting in a wheelchair in front of the TV, watching the preview guide roll by . . . over and over again. Tommy closed his eyes tight and swallowed; forcing back the sickening feeling that was welling up in him. He wished that he could go in and just hug his parents. He wished that he could help them. But he knew that he couldn't.

"Do you really know the price of becoming Irezumi, Tommy-san?"

TOMMY RENTED A small apartment in the downtown area. It wasn't in the sleazy part of town . . . But it was definitely in the seedy part of it. He was not slovenly and always kept his small rooms neat. He supported himself – working nights only – through occasional odd jobs. Nothing much. Just enough to keep him clothed, fed and sheltered. He did splurge on a few items, though. One was a large, full-length mirror, which he hung on the door. The other was dark, full-length curtains which he hung around the entire apartment to keep out the daylight. He had gotten used to living in a sort of solitary, *twilight world* . . .

and had, in time, come to accept it . . . To actually *embrace* it. He no longer cared for the sunny world outside of his Irezumi. It had become too bright, too glaring . . . too *harsh* . . . for him to bear.

Tommaso Tataglia now lived most of his life within his Irezumi . . . He had, for all intents and purposes, *become Irezumi.*

≈ ≈ ≈

ONE NIGHT, WHILE bored, and drinking just a little too heavily, in a downtown bar, Tommaso Tataglia was approached by a tall, gaunt man, wearing a rather garish, pin-stripped suit and white Panama hat, which he wore cocked to one side of his head.

"May I sit down?" the gaunt man asked.

Tommy looked down at the man's shoes – they were expensive, two-tone wingtips – and then up into the man's face. With his foot, he pushed back the chair across from him so that the man could sit.

"Thank you," the man said, as he seated himself. "My name is Levi."

He extended his hand to Tommy. Tommy did not respond. His gloved hands remained folded together on the table.

"I have been . . . admiring your . . . illustrations," the man said, after an awkward pause. "May I see you with your cap and glasses off?"

"What does he want," Tommy thought. *"A photo?"* Tommy hesitated for a moment and then, removed his cap and glasses.

The gaunt man stared. He seemed to be examining Tommy's face; much as a doctor would do.

42

"Beautiful," he said softly. "Simply beautiful. How much of your body do you have illustrated, may I ask?"

Tommy liked it when the man used the word 'illustrate'. "All of it," he answered.

The gaunt man stared at Tommy T. for a moment and then spoke. "I am a curator of . . . oddities," he began. "I am employed by a establishment that accrues and exhibits . . . unique and exceptional . . . objects of art."

He waited another moment and then he continued. "If the rest of your body is illustrated as beautifully as your face, I may have a . . . situation for you." The man remained calm when he spoke, and seemed to be earnest in what he said.

"Accrues and exhibits?" Tommy thought, trying to figure out the man's true meaning. *"He wants to buy a photo of me,"* he finally concluded.

"What kind of a situation," Tommy said.

"If you would accompany me to my hotel room, and allow myself and a colleague of mine to view the rest of your . . . illustration, I will explain my full intentions. Perhaps, over something to eat." He stared at Tommy for a moment. "I'm a bit hungry. How about you? Tommy did not respond. "Possibly," he went on, a bit stiffly, "after things are made a little clearer, we can come to an agreement in which all parties can be satisfied."

Tommy was low on funds, a little hungry, and had one more week until his rent was due.

"Let's go," he said.

≈ ≈ ≈

AT THE HOTEL the gaunt man introduced Tommy to his business associate. He, like the gaunt man, was polite and treated Tommy with much kindness. They ordered food and allowed Tommy to eat and shower before viewing his Irezumi.

Both men were impressed with what they saw. They explained the situation they had to offer to Tommy. It offered him a secure position and guaranteed that all of his needs would be met. The furnishing and decoration of his lodgings would be completely left up to him and paid for by his employer. He was told that, for as long as he was able to honor his 'small' part of the agreement, he would be taken care of in a manner that would be acceptable to him. The agreement that he had made with Horikin regarding the dispensation of his body would also be honored by his employer. There were some aspects of the situation that did not appeal to Tommy. But, on the whole, it was acceptable.

"Besides," he thought. *"It doesn't really matter anyway. I'll always be with my Irezumi."*

Tommy accepted the situation. "When do I start," he said.

The gaunt man took some papers from a briefcase, made any necessary additions and corrections that were needed, and asked Tommy to read them. If he agreed, he was to sign the revised agreement in the appropriate places. While waiting for the new contract to be typed up, the gaunt man booked Tommy a room at the hotel, gave him money to buy anything that he needed and took care of all the travel arrangements. Tommy read the new agreement and signed it. They left for Europe in three days.

≈ ≈ ≈

. . . Tommy rose from the dressing table, turned, and began walking toward the mirror situated in the corner on the other side of the room. Like the one on the dresser, it was three sided . . . But this one was life-sized and full length. The room was dark and completely surrounded with opaque, floor-to-ceiling curtains. There were no windows. The only light in the room came from the small bulbs that surrounded the mirror on the dresser; and the two large candles that were set on long metal pedestals, placed at either end of the room. The only sounds came from the stereo – which played only classical music – and the low whirring of the air conditioner – which was never turned off.

As he approached the mirror he undid the dressing gown; letting it fall behind him. His oiled body glistened with a subtle iridescence as he moved like a panther across the floor. When he reached the mirror, he stretched out his arm, switched on the track-lighting just above the mirror and stared at his magnificent body through the rich, amber-colored glow. At thirty seven he was still in good shape. His body still retained the firmness that it had in his youth.

Tommy was completely naked except for a thin, white, fundoshi *which covered his privates – if naked was what you could call it; for he was literally enveloped in a cocoon of bright color and shifting design. He stepped closer to the mirror and stared at himself intently. His entire body was a living mural. The golden carp, swimming through the deep blue-and-foam oceans covering each forearm were exact twins. The two red and green dragons, gliding fiercely through the angry grey*

45

clouds and bright yellow shafts of lightening which covered his biceps and triceps, were duplicates. Each shoulder possessed small, grey-black whorls that swept outward and grew larger as they traveled, like a dark whirlwind, down his chest. Coming to rest only when they reached the two large, flaming circles which covered his pectorals. Within each circle was the head of an angry, Japanese Warrior-God. The eyes were crossed; the faces fully made up in the traditional Kabuki fashion. Down and across his entire solar plexus, like a mammoth belt buckle, sat an enormous, sapphire colored Buddha. Its eyes were closed as it peacefully contemplated Nirvana. Its legs were folded serenely beneath flaxen robes. The hands gently held out a white Lotus blossom. Tommy's navel and the Buddha's were one. Below the Illustrious Buddha, in the nether regions of that astounding universe that quivered and swam around Tommy, was the ugly dwarfed head of a Chinese demon. Tommy undid the fundoshi and let it fall to the floor. The demon's distorted head was bright orange while its eyes gleamed a brilliant yellow. Its tongue – a fiery red – protruded profanely from its deformed mouth and wrapped itself around the full length of Tommy's penis.

Tommy then turned, looked up, and faced the slanted mirror that was hung from the ceiling. It was tilted at an angle that allowed him to view the back of his body through the large mirrors behind him. There, across the entire length and breath of his back, a Japanese warrior, with sword drawn, fought violently with an evil adversary. As Tommy flexed his back muscles and moved his torso and arms this way and that, the warrior came to life; wielding its heavy sword; dancing and stamping down on the enemy's head which lay beneath the warrior's large, sandaled feet. The rest of Tommy's body – Latisimus dorsi, buttocks, legs, hands, feet, face and neck – were covered with myriad mythical beings, elephants, tiny flowers and exotic birds.

Tommy turned around, faced the full-length mirrors and examined the front of himself again. With the exception of his back and chest, every illustration that was tattooed on one side of his body was meticulously and painstakingly reproduced on the other side. All the illustrations on his arms and legs faced towards the center of his body. "Perfect." He said again, softly. "Perfect." He thought of Bradbury's "The Illustrated Man", and of the part where the boy was lying down on the grass, gazing at the strange man's body: 'The pictures were moving,' the boy had said as he stared at the man's back, 'each in its turn, each for a brief minute or two.' "They are alive." Tommy said to himself as he stared at the swirling miasma before him in the mirror. "They are alive."

Tommaso Tataglia stood in front of the mirrors and watched with a strange delight as the two monkeys quarreled and bickered over a piece of fruit that one of them had snatched from underneath his hair line. He giggled as the twin carp placidly slid through the swirling waters around his arms. He listened, and thought he could almost hear, the two gods in the flaming circles on his chest discussing war strategies. Elephants bellowed. Serpents hissed. Lightening crashed. The Illustrious Buddha pronounced the Sacred 'Om'. Adrift in his *own universe, Tommy T. stood in front of the mirrors and smiled benevolently at his subjects.*

A LOUD KNOCK at the door caused Tommy T. to flinch. The small shock drove him back to the present.

"Five minutes kid," a crusty voice hollered from the other side of the door.

Tommy turned, picked up his fundoshi and kimono, and walked back to the dressing table. He tied up the fundoshi and slid the robe on over his shoulders; tying the silk sash into a neat knot around his waist. He picked up the cigarette that he had placed in the ashtray. It had gone out. He flicked the lighter on the silver cigarette case and lit it.

"Ladie-e-e-e-s . . . and gentlemen!" He heard the barker shout. "For your expres-s-s-s-s enjoyment and pleasure . . . Recently back from his European tour-r-r-r . . . The world's most *tat* to-o-o-o-ed man . . . Ladie-e-e-e-e-s and gentleman . . . Sir-r-r-r Thomas of Constantine!"

The door to his dressing room swung inward; bringing with it the flashy, orange glow of carnival lighting. He could hear the loud, mechanically-musical sound of the carousel as it whirled round and round. He heard the laughing and screaming of the crowds. The pungently-sweet smell of popcorn, cotton candy and caramel drifted into his nostrils and settled onto the tip of his tongue. Tommaso Tataglia took one more puff on his cigarette, blew the smoke out hard, crushed the cigarette in the silver dragon ashtray and stepped out onto the viewing platform.

EPILOGUE

While in his ninth year with the circus, Tommy T. began to experience abdominal pains. He was examined by a physician and told that exploratory surgery would be required to correctly diagnose the problem.

≈ ≈ ≈

On a chilly night in December, three months after his medical consultation, Tommaso Tataglia died, apparently peacefully, in his sleep.

His will, meticulously drawn up under the supervision of a very distinguished and highly successful Japanese attorney – who, by the way, was also *Irezumi,* and a member of Horikin's Nakama – stated that, in the event of his demise, Tommaso Tataglia's body was, in no way, to undergo an autopsy until it had first been returned to Japan. However, a blood sample was allowed and no toxins were discovered in his system. The will also stated that, upon his death, a certain Mitsuaki Ohwada be contacted immediately to dispose of the body. Within two days, Horikin arrived from Japan to claim and recover Tommy's body.

≈ ≈ ≈

Tommy T.'s body was flown back to Sagami and taken to Horikin's studio. His entire Irezumi was then carefully and meticulously removed from his body. It was spread out and slowly cured and oiled until it was as pliant as butter. The Irezumi was then carefully wrapped in a bolt of red silk and placed into one of the large teakwood chests in

49

Horikin's studio – along with the other hundred or so Irezumi that had been amassed through the years by Horikin and the members of his Nakama – for private viewing.

On every anniversary of the completion of the illustration of Tommy T., Horikin carefully unwraps Tommy's Irezumi and lays it out for display to the remaining disciples of his Nakama. He pours them all hot sake from a black porcelain, dragon-decorated decanter. They raise their cups and drink a toast . . . In honor of the Irezumi . . . and also to the two thousand year old art of the *Horishi* . . . the body illustrators.

THE GIFT

It's four thirty in the morning. The streets are all but empty. The old man is packing his equipment into his dilapidated '67 Caddie. It used to be a rich hunter's green but now, after many grueling years on the road, its true color is unidentifiable . . . It is non-colored.

It's the same routine after every gig. National steel guitar in the back seat, harps and rack on the front, and amp, mic and mic stand in the trunk. Just before he gets in the car he stands, faces the now deserted club, and performs the usual 'idiot check': "Mic, stand, amp, guitar, harps, cords? Got everything? OK," he says to no one in particular, "Let's roll."

As he stares at the front of the vacant club, he catches his reflection in one of the blacked-out windows. He looks a little tired . . . and "just a little bit older", he thinks, than yesterday. He frowns at first, and then, smoothing back his thick, steely-grey mane, smiles widely, displaying his one gold-oval-crowned, capped tooth. For just a split second it glints brilliantly back at him. "Well, 'least I ain't bald," he says, in a somewhat wry voice. ". . .Yet," he adds.

He turns, opens the Caddie's dent-scarred door, eases in behind the wheel, and attempts to crank up the battered, rust-and-oil-encrusted engine. She grinds around a few times, threatening to start, but then cuts out. He pumps the gas five times – the usual ritual – jams his foot down hard on the accelerator, forces the ignition key all the way to the right, and holds it there.

"Come on, baby . . . Come on, girl wake up," he mutters impatiently. "Time to go."

At first she resists – she's a little tired too – but, then, realizing there is no way out, she coughs, sputters a bit and, with a final, defiant wheeze, drops down into a smooth hum. The old man smiles, pats the dash affectionately, shifts into drive, and rumbles away from the curb – power steering unit squealing wildly – to find the highway and the next gig.

When he reaches the entrance to the freeway he pushes down on the accelerator. The disheveled machine lurches forward, climbs the ramp, and is gone – leaving a viperous cloud of partially ignited cheap gas and oil in its wake.

When the dog-weary Caddie reaches sixty – and nothing blows up or flies off – the old man relaxes. He glances down at the crumpled map lying on the front seat and pulls down the itinerary that is stuck up in the sun shield. He rustles and flattens out the map with one hand until he sees the red ballpoint circle he is searching for. Then he picks up the itinerary – scanning the list of club names and addresses until he comes to the name that matches the one on the map.

The club is named the Scarlet D. It's in Mifflinburg, PA – about three hundred miles from his present location. "Better drive straight on through," he says out loud. "I'll get some sleep when I pull in," he adds – Being alone so much, he has gotten into the habit of talking out loud to himself. "No sense sleepin' in this burg. My leg feels like it might rain (that fight he got into down in that club in Algiers) an' these wipers ain't workin' too good either . . . 'Specially the right one."

≈ ≈ ≈

After a half an hour or so, the old man begins to settle into the groove. He pulls a pack of Pall Malls from his shirt pocket, fishes one out, flips the pack up onto the cluttered dash, and presses the lighter button above the butt-choked ashtray. In about twenty seconds he hears it pop.

"It's a wonder that damn thing still works," he mumbles as he presses the glowing coil up against the tip of the cigarette. "Nothin' else does." The radio, power seats, and windows have all died a merciful death years ago.

He taps the burnt strands of tobacco from the lighter coil and pushes it back into its sheath. While taking a long pull on the cigarette, he casually glances up. From the faint radiance given off by the cigarette's 'cherry', he catches his reflection in the rear view mirror. He is still wearing his shades. He carefully removes them and slides them into his shirt pocket. Then he reaches over, snaps open the glove compartment, pulls out a silver, half-pint flask of Wild Turkey, cracks the lid, and squeezes off a swig.

"Ahhh," he hisses, as he feels the hot liquid running down his dry throat and into his belly. He returns the flask, slams the glove compartment door closed, and takes another long, hard drag on his Pall Mall – allowing the grey smoke to trickle slowly out of his nose.

He is a bluesman. Plays bluesharp, slideguitar and sings the blues . . . 'Down Home' blues, to be precise. He's close to sixty now, and has been playing blues for the past forty. He has performed in just about every blues club in just about every city in these United States . . . And a few in Canada and Europe too. In his younger days, at the beginning of his career, he enjoyed going 'on the road' – traveling from club to club and city to city. Every gig was a new adventure for him then. But now, after all these years, it all just comes natural. It's his way of life now. Almost like a reflex. But he still loves the blues – and that's what keeps him traveling from town to town, singing and playing. That . . . And "lookin'" . . .

"Gotta keep lookin'," he says to himself, while staring steadfastly at the road ahead. "Gonna find 'im one of these nights . . . Just gotta keep lookin'. 'Least that's what the old man told me."

As he searches back into his mind, he can almost hear that old man's scruffy voice . . . As clear as if he was still sitting there – right next to him in the truck: 'Keep lookin', Son,' the voice said, 'You'll find 'im. You'll know it's the right one when ya look 'im in the eye. Butcha gotta keep lookin', Son, jus' like I did.'

The miles start rolling by under his wheels. The old bluesman shoulders himself deeper into his seat and yawns. As the white strips in the road slip past him, he begins to think of how it all began . . . How it all began those many years ago in that tin-roofed juke joint on a hot Saturday night down in the Mississippi Delta. His mind begins to drift back. Back some forty odd years in time . . . To that night when he received the Gift . . .

≈ ≈ ≈

It was the summer of '51. The boy had just turned nineteen. He and a friend of his were spending the summer drifting around through the southern United States in an old pick up truck. They had no set thought or destination in mind. Just driving for the hell of it. They had purchased the truck – a beat-up nineteen forty-three Ford – for eighty dollars. It was dented and rusty, but the engine was sound and ran like a clock.

They traveled to Virginia, then through the Carolinas to Alabama and Louisiana. Then they circled back down to Mississippi. Just "drivin', drinkin' in the sights an' diggin' the blues."

Both of the boys dug the blues, and would stop at every juke joint and honky-tonk they came upon just to hear those ol' bluesmen "layin' it down". His friend loved the blues – but the boy *really* loved them. It seemed as though he could never get enough. At every club they'd hit, you would always find the boy: seated right at a front table . . . spellbound in the blues.

The rural south was different in those days. Acre upon acre of fertile farmland, cut through by miles and miles of winding dirt roads. Shotgun houses precariously perched on three foot high cinder block supports dotted the landscape. Some of those houses were so flimsy, and tilted so badly over to one side, that they needed to be shored-up with two-by-fours to keep them from toppling completely over.

As the two boys drove past some of these modest dwellings they would occasionally spot an old man or two sitting on the rickety wooden porch lazily playing blues or gospel on a beat up Martin or a rusty old National, while using the broken neck of a whiskey bottle as a slide. The two boys would pull over and sit there – just watching those old timers perform. Some played blues on a homemade *Diddly-Bo*. Some were blowing "low down an' dirty" on a fifty-cent Marine Band. Some had even made "*git*-tars" out of wooden cigar boxes, using a piece of old piano wire for a string. They could slide up and down that one wire with a bottleneck slide and make it sound just like a store bought instrument. The boys saw bluesmen slapping on basses made from washtubs and mop handles, using a piece baling twine for the string.

It was the time when juke joints, as well as general stores sold mason jars of "White Lightnin'" for fifty cents a pint.

≈ ≈ ≈

It was all a great experience. But, like I said before, the boy just couldn't seem to get enough. The more blues he heard, the more he wanted to hear. He'd go to see a band and listen, or maybe sit in for a tune or two, if they let him – he *did* sing a little and play some harp too. Nothing big, though. But . . . thinking back . . . he wasn't *just* listening . . . He was also *looking*. Looking for something that, at that time, he couldn't define. Something that he just couldn't put his finger on – but that was *turning in its sleep* deep down in his soul. It was as if a finite *entity* was germinating deep within his very being . . . Like a final *Puzzle-Piece* was gradually being affixed to his core, or . . . Life-Force, as it were.

He didn't know it at the time, but that boy was getting ready to meet the blues . . . *In* person.

Now, like I said before, the boy did sing a little, and also play some harp at the time. But nothing big. Just 'sittin' in' every once in a while with bands that let him, or 'squeakin' on his harp while his friend was driving the rig – *which sometimes had the tendency to work on his friend's last nerve.*

He could always remember the first time he had heard the blues. He was just a kid . . . ten or twelve maybe. His mom had bought him a crystal radio for Christmas. Those type radios didn't need a battery – or to be plugged in either. And they could only be listened to through headphones. One night he was in his bed playing with the channels when, all of a sudden, he heard . . .

"You got me peepin', you got me hidin'
You got me peep, hide . . . hide peep
Any way you want it, let it roll
Yeah . . . yeah . . . yeah,
You got me doin' what you want me
Now, baby, what you want me to do."

That was his first taste of the blues. The late, great Jimmy Reed. And the name of that show – which he never forgot – was *The Night Owl*. It aired Monday through Friday, from 10:30 to 11:00 PM. Somehow, despite his age, that music touched his young soul. Every night he'd jump into bed and force himself to stay awake until 10:30 – no matter *how* tired he was – so that he could tune in *The Night Owl*. It became a fundamental part of his nightly routine. Jimmy Reed, Son House, Howlin' Wolf, Tarheel Slim, Mississippi Fred McDowell . . . All the blues legends were aired on that show.

It wasn't too long after listening to the Night Owl, that he purchased his first Marine Band harmonica. He came across a box of them while looking around in an old pawnshop downtown, and just had to have one. It took him a while but, after almost driving everyone around him half crazy with his squeaking and "hee-hawing", he finally learned to play something that could be classified as music.

So you see, even back then he had it . . . A tiny seed . . . just waiting for some water.

≈ ≈ ≈

It was one of those sticky Saturday afternoons – typical in the Mississippi Delta at that time of year – and the two boys were bouncing along one of those old dirt backroads that were so common then. The road was parched and dry from baking in the hot Delta sun all day – causing immense clouds of red dust to rise from the truck's rotating rear wheels. The clouds grew larger and larger, until the only thing that could be seen through the rear view mirror were billows of densely thick, ginger colored dust. The cotton was in full bloom along both sides of the road for as far as the eye could see. When you drove past one of the fields during the day, even though it was summer, it looked as though it had just snowed. The only sounds that were audible besides the random screeching of a few crows, and the low grinding of an occasional tractor, came from field hands . . . Singing . . . to forget how hard their days on this earth were. It seemed as though their work songs could be heard for miles and miles across the flat, fertile Delta countryside. To the boy, they were a prayer. He could almost see them . . . drifting lazily into the heavens like waves of heat . . . and then melting, like warmed butter, just as they reached the sizzling Delta sun. The boy felt that he could just sit there and listen to those songs forever.

From behind the wheel of his battered machine the old man smiles to himself, thinking of how it was in those days. He lights another cigarette, brings the flask out, takes another sip, and sighs heavily.

In his mind's eye, he can still see the scorching Delta sun setting on that particular night. It was a giant, shimmering ball of red fire – balanced directly on the horizon. Sitting . . . like a fat, complacent Buddha . . . exactly on the rim of the earth. It appeared to be almost three times its actual size. Its crimson glow was so intense that everything else in view was transformed into a pitch-black silhouette. Trees, flying birds . . . Everything. He remembers that he was so impressed by the sight that he had asked his friend to stop the truck so that he could get out and take a better look . . .

≈ ≈ ≈

As the boy stood and watched the sun slowly sinking behind a dark mass of Sycamore trees, it seemed to him, for just a moment or two, that the entire earth itself had become engulfed in a mysterious, mandarin tinted luminescence.

Just then he experienced a strange sensation. Something appeared to be pressing in from behind him. He quickly turned. Nothing. Then he looked up. To his left and above, he saw the full moon, rising slowly into the heavens. It had the appearance and texture of an

59

enormous, yellow, hard-boiled egg yoke. And then . . . as quickly as it had appeared . . . that glowing red coal that was the sun, dipped below the horizon and was snuffed out. The mysterious crimson-colored world faded and . . . in the twinkling of an eye . . . it was night.

While he stood in the darkness, a shivery breeze passed over his body – carrying with it an inhospitable chill. He suddenly felt cold . . . and alone. A verse from an old blues song he had once heard slowly drifted into his head . . .

> *"Well, the moon is risin'*
> *An' the sun have done gone down*
> *Hell Hound's on my trail*
> *Yeah, I'm gonna have to leave this town."*

It was then that he felt that first odd physical sensation. The feeling seemed to be entering his body through the soles of his feet. It was a strange *humming*; rushing, full-tilt, right up both of his legs. It shot straight up his back, down his arms, and then straight up his neck to the top of his head.

The night began to feel odd . . . wild . . . *Primeval*. The boy then began to sense an even stranger sensation. A kind of *rhythm* . . . thrumming its way up from the road. It felt as though it was actually *oozing* up through his shoes and twisting around his body like a wild, pulsing vine. Fear gripped his heart. He turned on his heel, quickly ran back to the truck, and jumped, slamming the door behind him with a hard thud.

"Take off!" he said loudly, alarmed and frightened.

"What's the matter?" his friend answered, puzzled by the boy's actions.

"Take off!" the boy shouted this time. " . . . An' gimme that bottle!" He could feel his heart hammering hard against his ribs.

His friend slammed the engine into gear. Gravel shot up from the rear tires, pelting the undersides of the fenders, and the truck took off down the road – weaving helter-skelter like a spooked possum. The bright yellow beams from the headlights bounced wildly up and down as the tires jolted through mud holes – cutting a frenzied swath through the inky night.

≈ ≈ ≈

It took awhile for the boy to calm down. But, even though he had relaxed – in addition to the whiskey numbing his senses a bit – he could still feel that eerie vibration coursing through his body. And then . . . as they proceeded further down that desolate road . . . he began to *hear* something too. He looked nervously over at his friend: "Hear that?"

His friend stared back at him for a few seconds and then said, "Cool out, man . . . Everything's OK." But the glint in his friend's eyes betrayed his true feelings. His friend was beginning to wonder if the boy *was* "OK", or *not* . . . And the boy could clearly see that.

That's when the boy realized that his friend wasn't feeling or hearing anything . . . It was just him.

The further down the road they traveled, the more distinct the pattern of the beat became. Then he actually started thinking that he heard someone singing. But it all seemed to be happening inside his own head. A gritty, rusty old voice seemed to be mumbling . . . or chanting to him. With every turn of the odometer the elegy became clearer and clearer . . . until he could distinctly hear the words that were being sung . . .

> *"Well, I dreamed I was a catfish*
> *Swimmin' in the deep blue sea,*
> *I had all you pretty woman*
> *Fishin' after me.*
> *Oh, Well . . . Sho' 'nuf, I did,*
> *Oh, Lord . . . Sho' 'nuf, I did."*

A shiver ran through him and all the hairs on his body bristled. He was just about to take another shot of Wild Turkey when, over to his right, he saw a narrow, one lane, deeply rutted dirt road. It appeared to wind right through the cotton field. The 'sound' appeared to be coming from that direction. And it seemed to be beckoning – *summoning* – him towards it.

"Turn off here," he said abruptly, pointing to the road.

His friend gave a quick start, scudded on the brakes, swung the truck right and, with a sudden jolt of the springs, headed down that side road into the sullen, ebony night. Voluminous clouds of white dust sailed up in their wake like rooster tails on a speedboat.

Recovering from the initial shock, his friend gave the boy a worried glance and said, "What the hell's with you, man. You all right?'

"Just follow the road", he answered, taking another gulp of whiskey. His mouth had become dry and he was feeling a little *trembley* all over.

≈ ≈ ≈

As they drove on, the boy observed a faint glow coming from the other side of the field . . . Shimmering far off in the distance and to the left. It was pale and ghostly . . Like a tiny ember flickering feebly in a waning fire. He could hear the music more clearly now and, once again, his hair bristled.

"Head for that light," he said, pointing in that direction.

They rode on, twisting and turning, until, as the truck cornered one of the bends, a clearing suddenly appeared. And in the center of it stood a long, low cabin. Right out in the middle of, what seemed to be, nowhere. The truck slowed down as the boy's friend urged it up under a tree. He gunned the motor and then switched off the ignition. They both sat there . . . Just staring . . .

It was a low wooden shack with a tin roof. It had a covered porch that ran across its entire length. As there eyes got more used to the dark, they could see partially rusted-away tin signs, nailed haphazardly across the front of the place. There was a giant soda cap with *Coca-Cola* scrolled across it. A red winged horse with a banner in its teeth advertised *Mobil* A barely visible sign promoting *Dixie Peach Hair Pomade* hung at a precarious angle – slanting over another one that had long since become unreadable.

A few men were sitting around on the porch talking. Others leaned idly against the porch beams drinking 'Shine. In the outer darkness, other men were also standing; conversing amongst themselves, or quietly chatting with women.

The boy looked up. The pallid light of the moon was captured by the tin roof, causing it to glint and shimmer – giving it the false illusion of movement. All the doors and windows were slung wide open – allowing a luminous yellow light . . . along with the distinct odor of kerosene . . . to escape into the night air. Fly strips hung in the doorways and windows, swaying slowly in the breeze, gravely displaying their cadaverous bounty of flies, mosquitoes and beetles. Someone inside was singing a blues song. It drifted slowly through the windows and doors. It seemed to stop and dangle right in front of the boy.

At first, the men on the porch just sat there eyeing the two boys with vaguely suspicious stares. It was as if they were trying to fathom what two strangers were doing way down here in the *Foggy Bottom* . . . And at this hour, no less.

At last one of the bolder men spoke up. "You boys lost?"

For an instant the entire scene seemed to freeze. The talking ceased. The music stopped. Everyone and everything appeared to solidify. Even the gentle swaying of the Spanish moss in the Sycamore trees and the boisterous chirping of the crickets hidden in the grass came to an abrupt halt. All was stilled . . . All except for, what sounded like, an old gospel song . . . being sung far off and in the distance . . .

"Well, you better hush . . .
Yes, you better hush . . .
'Cause somebody's callin' your name.
Oh my Lord . . . Oh my Lord,

Who can it be . . ."
Did everyone hear it? . . . Or was it just meant
for the boy . . .

"We came to listen to the music," the boy finally responded, still a bit shaken from his strange experience. "We could hear it from the main road."

Through the dim light he could see the taut stances of the men begin to relax. And then . . . in an instant . . . everything snapped back into motion. People started talking, the music began once again, and the crickets began to chirp.

Immediately the boy felt his anxiety vanish like a bad dream at sunrise. He swung open the truck door and jumped down off the running board onto the grass – causing the truck's travel-worn springs to squeal loudly.

"Okay if we go in?" He asked, pointing to the open door of the juke joint.

One of the men sitting on the porch absently sipping *'Shine* from his Mason jar said, "Go 'head on in, Junebug. Ain't nobody gonna bother ya".

The two boys walked across the hard-packed dirt that covered the front of the place, hopped onto the dilapidated wooden porch, and stood in the doorway, looking in. A few heads turned, like they did outside, but then all returned to normal.

The inside of the place was relatively bare of furniture: Five or six wooden tables – complemented by odd-matched chairs – were scattered here and there throughout the room. Near the back wall a few wide planks laid across two barrels served as the bar. Sawdust was scattered across the floor. The place was lit by kerosene lanterns.

A few couples were seated at the tables quietly conversing. Every so often one of the men would whisper, with a sly look in his eye, into his woman's ear – causing the mellow atmosphere of the room to explode with a shrill laugh, or a loud, giggly, "*Hush*, Fool!" Three or four couples were dancing in the middle of the sawdust strewn dance floor. One or two of them glanced idly in the boys' direction, but then went back to the business of partying. Wooden benches lined one side of the room. They were mostly occupied by older men, just sitting around smoking pipes and small-talking. Two of the men had a dog-eared checkerboard laid between them. As they slammed down the chipped disks they issued such aphorisms as: "Ha! Ha! *Gotcha*, Boy!" or, "*Look out*, Baby, 'cause you jus' phoned yo' Aunt Jane!" Out through the back door the boy could hear the distinct clatter of dice being pitched against the wall – along the sharp snap of fingers. Unseen voices shouted "Hot *Damn!*" or, "*No*, Baby! Don't hide it . . . *Dee-vide* it!" It was the usual good-natured clamor of common folk unwinding after a hard week's work out in the hellish Delta sun.

But the sound that particularly caught the boy's attention was the rhythmic slapping of a shoe on the wooden floor, the rusty whine produced by a bottleneck slide being hauled up and down the strings of a steel guitar – and the wintry voice that accompanied it. He slowly glanced around the room. Over in a far corner, he beheld the source of his curiosity . . .

He was an extremely thin, and delicately frail, old

man. His skin was the color of burnished ebony. His slender fingers resembled thin, brittle sticks as they nimbly worked their way up and down the strings of an ancient, rusted, *National* steel guitar he had cradled in his lap. On his left pinkie he sported a green, glass, bottleneck slide. He was toothless, except for one gold-capped left incisor, and had a two-day, snow-white stubble sprouting from his chin. His eyes were red and set deep in his archaic head. They had the appearance of two embers; glowing within a dark cave. He wore a dark, blue serge, pin-striped suit, which shined from too much pressing, and a white dress shirt – unbuttoned at the neck and frayed at the wrists and collar. From the open part of his shirt a small, black, silk bag could be seen. It hung flat – sticking to his sweaty chest – from a twisted leather thong. He wore a large, 'Apple Jack' cap that sat *Acey Ducey* on his gaunt head. On his feet, he wore a pair of black, high-topped 'ol' man comforts' . . . Worn and cracked, but highly polished.

The boy stared at the old man – Hypnotized by what he saw and heard – Held captive by the haunting strains of the old man's chanting lament.

The old man never stopped playing. The tune appeared, at times, to be on the verge of terminating . . . One second . . . Two . . . Then the bottleneck would slide back up the strings of the rusty old guitar – building the music back up to a screaming vibrato that was amplified by the guitar's metal resonators . . .

"Well, engineer blow yo' whistle
An' firemen ring yo' bell

Well, I ain't got time
Ta bid ma' baby fare thee well."

The boy was drawn straight into the music that this strange old man was playing. As if in a trance – and before he even knew what he was doing – the boy found himself sitting right in front of this odd, and eccentrically clad, bluesman. He sat backwards on a beat up wooden chair with his legs spread wide across the seat and his arms absently folded over its back – staring straight at the old man.

The boy was so captivated by the music that he didn't even notice his friend slip up beside him and ask if he wanted a drink. When the boy didn't answer his friend nudged him gently on the shoulder, finally breaking his concentration.

"Hey, man, you want a beer or somethin'?"

"Yeah, OK," he answered, without even bothering to look up.

A frosty bottle of *Dixie* was brought back and pushed against his arm.

"Thanks," he mumbled, still staring at the old man. He took a sip and placed the sweating bottle between his legs on the chair.

Without even ending his previous song, the bluesman broke into Robert Johnson's Crossroads:

"I went down to the crossroad,
Fell down on my knees . . .
Asked the Lord above have mercy,

Help po' Bob, if you please."

The boy was in total awe of, what he termed, this bluesman's *"Soul"*.

"What I wouldn't give to sing and play like that," thought the boy. *"If I could play the blues like that, I'd never stop."*

The boy was so caught up with the singing and slide playing that it took him awhile to realize that the old man was staring at him. Their eyes met and the youth was locked into the old man's riveting gaze. It seemed to the boy, by the way he was being eyed, that the old man knew him, and was just on the verge of saying something to him . . . But he didn't. He just kept on singing . . . All the while staring straight into the boy's eyes.

As the boy gazed deeper and deeper into the old man's fiery red eyes, the room and all the people in it, slowly faded into a foggy, grey mist. The mist grew darker and heavier until it appeared that all that was left in the entire universe were just two small, glowing red coals – and a strange, pulsing, primeval rhythm that seemed as ancient as the dawn of man itself.

As the boy closed his eyes he felt as though he was being transported back in time . . . Back to the beginning . . . the very *inception* of mans' comprehension of, what we, for lack of a better description, call Rhythm . . . or *Soul* . . .

≈ ≈ ≈

When the swirling mists within his mind slowly began to clear, the boy saw Ancient Man – squatting dirty and naked on a barren, primal shore. His shaggy, unkempt head was cocked to one side. He appeared to be listening to the rhythmic crashing of the waves, the lonely whistling of the wind raking across the sand . . . and all the other myriad sounds made by Nature's infinite creations. Then, before his eyes, the boy saw this primitive being begin to change. He ceased to just listen . . . He now began to imitate the sounds that he was hearing. First, by just humming badly while clumsily tapping on the ground with a stick. And then, as time began moving at a faster pace, Ancient Man refined the crude humming and tapping into a meaningful, more articulate form of expression. A form of expression that would soon be shared by . . . and then unite . . . first small bands, then tribes . . . and finally whole civilizations . . . of people. The boy then saw men, women and children . . . all moving, swinging and swaying in unison . . . He saw them dancing, beating on drums, strumming on stringed instruments and blowing through hollowed reeds. Whole societies . . . all moving as one unit. Rocking, singing, stamping their feet. All one component . . . All moving in one cadence . . . All dancing along with the Great Soul of the Universe.

≈ ≈ ≈

As time began to advance even more swiftly before the boy's eyes, the youth then saw that the more 'civilized' man became, the less he was in tune with the natural vibrations of the heavens. He saw that the further man moved from his natural *soulfulness,* the less he was able to experience that rhythm, that *Subtle Essence,* that had once been an essential part of his existence. Further and further man separated himself until, in the end, the Gift that was once given to him by the Gods, was all but abandoned – lost in the dark, hazy mists of the past.

Those few individuals who still *did* possess the ability to comprehend this natural 'cadence of life', and were able to communicate it – whether vocally or with the aid of an instrument – to the rest of mankind . . . Those that *did* . . . Those that had the capability to reach down into other folks' souls and awaken them . . . were acknowledged by the general masses as talented . . . or *Gifted*.

Whether they were performing a piece by Wagner in a palatial stadium before thousands or, like the old bluesman . . . just singing blues in some remote honky-tonk for maybe forty people . . . it was all the same. They *moved* people . . . People *felt* them. These *Gifted Ones* had the ability to awaken an emotional response deep down inside others which had, through the passing of time . . . and neglect . . . become all but dormant. Those with the *Gift* had the ability to reach inside a person and awaken the *Soul* in them. And, for a short while, bring them back into sync with the Pulse of Creation.

All this – and more . . . *much* . . . much more – washed across the field of vision in the boy's mind as he sat listening to this old man playing the blues in a tin-roofed honky-tonk down in the Delta on a hot, sticky, Mississippi Saturday night.

≈ ≈ ≈

How much time had passed since the young man first sat down he could not say. But, as quickly as it had appeared, the vision faded. He looked up, trying to focus his thoughts, and there stood the old man, right in front of him . . . guitar slung over his right shoulder . . . a gentle smile on his care-lined face.

As the room grew more focused, the boy realized that

the old man was speaking to him. "Can you give me a lift, Son?' he was saying softly.

The boy turned his head and looked around the room. The juke joint was empty. Through the open window he could see the brilliant full moon moving on its random course through the sky.

The boy smiled at the old bluesman, stood up, stretched, and rubbed his eyes sleepily. The old man handed him the guitar. He took it, slung it over his shoulder and, before he even realized what he was doing, him and the old man were both walking toward the truck.

Looking around the yard and not seeing anyone, the boy asked, "Where's my friend?"

"Don't worry 'bout him, Son," said the old man, slowly stepping up onto the running board with a grunt. "He's fine. It's you an' me that's got to be hurryin' on. Got to make it home a'fore that rooster crow," he said, as he slid into the cab and slammed the door shut with a jolt.

For just an instant, the boy became suspicious of the old man and fear began to slip into his heart. But just one look into the old man's face quelled all his apprehensions. He somehow knew that everything was going to be all right. With that settled in his mind, he climbed into the truck and slammed the door closed. He twisted the key and pumped gas. The engine grumbled resentfully a few times and then, with a weak sputter, came to life.

"Which way?" He asked dully – still not fully aware of the dream-like state that he was in.

"Straight down yonder between them trees, Son. I'll tell ya where to turn from there."

As they rumbled down the rutted dirt road the old

man turned and stared at the youth for a second or two. Then he shook his head and let out a soft chuckle.

"I know'd I'd feel ya when ya finally came along," he said, "but I sure didn't expect ya to just walk right up an' sit down in front of me like ya did tonight. Thought I'd hafta go lookin' for ya. Yes, the Lord sho works in mysterious ways, Son. He *sho'* does. *Um, Um, Um!*" he concluded, slowly shaking his head again.

"What do you mean?" the boy said, a little puzzled.

"You'll see, Son. You'll see. I got somethin' for ya. Somethin' I got ta give ya." He looked at the boy, shook his head, smiled peculiarly, and made that same soft chuckling sound once again.

The boy stared hard at the old man. Once again, he became disturbed by the old bluesman's actions.

"What's he up to," he thought to himself. *"He might be crazy an' try to pull a razor on me or somethin'."*

He was just about to slam on the brakes and reach under the seat for the bumper jack, when the old man spoke up abruptly. "Pull over there, boy. Right under them trees . . . An' cut the engine."

Like a zombie, blindly obeying his Voodoo master, the youth pulled over, gunned the engine and switched off the key.

As the boy turned and stared into the old man's face, he noticed that the old man looked a little older and frailer than he did at the club. In an instant, he knew that the old man wasn't out to hurt him. His fears dispersed, he exhaled deeply and relaxed.

The old man gazed at the boy for a long while. He appeared to be struggling with something he wanted to say

. . . Something that seemed to be sitting there, right on the tip of his tongue . . . but had become stuck.

After a lengthy pause the old man spoke . . .

"Son," he said, "I'm gonna tell you a story an' I don't want you to say nothin' 'till I'm finished, 'cause we ain't got too much time."

He glanced out the fly spattered window and peeped up at the sky. It was neither day nor night. The entire sky appeared to have turned into a cold, dark steely-grey cap. A troubled look clouded the old man's wrinkled face. He hesitated for another moment, then turned to the boy and continued.

"Many years ago," he said, "can't recollect exactly how long . . . was about your age, I reckon . . . I was walkin' home down a dark, dirt road. I was comin' back from a juke joint. Played some guitar at the time. Nothin' big, now . . . just some stuff my uncle had showed me . . . He played pretty good slide, my uncle did. Well, anyway, that particular night I was sittin' in with this band I knew. They'd buy me a beer once in awhile, or maybe a fish san'wich, but that's all. Well, I'm walkin' home, like I said, when I hear a groanin' comin' from the side of the road. Like I said, it was dark . . . darker than it is now . . . so I couldn't make out who or what was causin' that sound. But I followed them groans 'till I come upon a man lyin' in the ditch. When I bent down close to 'im, I could see that he was in pretty bad shape. Appeared to be shot or stabbed, or somethin'. Couldn't tell which. All I knew was that he was gaspin' for air pretty hard. Anyway, when I bent closer to see if I could help him, he grabbed me by the collar of my shirt, pulled me real close to his face, an' stared me straight in my eyes. That man's eyes were as big as silver dollars, Son. Almost scared me half to death, he did. But then, as he stared at me, a look of relief seemed to come over him an' a feeble smile spread across his lips. 'Never thought I'd find ya, boy,' he whispered at me, 'but the Lord works his magic. Yes, He does.' Yes, that's what he told me. Then he coughed up a little bit of blood an' went on. 'I ain't got too much time left, boy,' he says to me, 'so jus' come close to me an' listen good.' Then he told me . . . jus' like I'm tellin' you right now . . . 'bout how, when he was a young, strugglin' musician, he was approached by an old bluesman that give him, what he called, the *Gift*. At first I thought he was in a delirium from his wound . . . or jus' plain ol' crazy . . . Like you must be thinkin' 'bout me right now, Son. (The old man chuckled a bit to himself and then continued.)

"He told me that this Gift he received was somethin' that had been passed down through the ages – from one generation to another. It started so far back in time that the man that give it to him didn't even know how, or when the *givin'* first began. Called it the *Gift of Rhythm*. Told me that the man that give it to him said that it was only a sort of a loan. Said it could be *used*, but couldn't be *kept*. Said it had to be passed on to the next generation. An' that he was the one had been chose to do the *passin'*. That old man told 'im that he would know who the right one was to pass it on to jus' by lookin' 'im in the eye.

"Then that dyin' man pulled me close, whispered somethin' in my ear, took me by the head an' blew somethin' in my mouth. Shortly after that, Son, he went limp an' passed.

"I jumped up an' ran all the way home. Scared to death. An' I didn't sleep a wink all night. Next mornin' I went back to that ditch with my uncle, but the man was gone. I searched all around but couldn't even find a drop a blood to prove that he was there.

"Never even know'd his name, Son, but I know that he did give me somethin' that night . . . He give me the *Gift* . . . An' I been usin' it ever since. It brought happiness to me as well as others. Carried me into some strange and wondrous places and situations, it did . . . Yes, it *sho'* did. (the old man chuckled again.) But lookin' back, Son, it made my life a better one to live. An' I'm proud that I was chosen. Yes, Son, I'd say that I was *blessed* by it."

The old man turned and glanced up at the sky one more time. A fretful look appeared on his face. He turned back to the boy once again.

"Yes, Son," he continued, "I was blessed with the Gift, an' I had it for many years now, like I told ya . . . But now it's time for me to pass it on. An' you the one I'm choosin' to pass it on to."

He looked fondly at the youth for a moment. It was almost as if he was proud of this boy . . . This boy that he had known for only one night . . . One short night in his long, hard life. He smiled at the boy. "Yeah, Son . . . you the one."

The old man then reached out, gently took the boy by the collar, pulled him close and began whispering in his ear.

The words – or *incantation*, if you like – that were spoken that night, I cannot repeat in this narration. The boy was also instructed to repeat them just *once* . . . And only where and when the time was right.

As the old man continued whispering, the truck began to spin slowly outward in a wide arc. The truck began to turn faster and faster on its axis with each rotation. The view from the windshield was quickly becoming a blurry mass. Spinning . . . Spinning . . . Spinning. Wider and wider.

It was then that the boy heard the song . . . Drifting in amidst the swirling chaos . . .

"Well, I dreamed I was a catfish
Swimmin' in the deep blue sea
I had all you pretty women
Fishin' after me
Oh, Well . . . Sho' 'nuff, I did
Oh, Lord . . . Sho' 'nuff, I did."

The song went on and on . . . Verse after verse. The world spun on and on. Spinning and spinning. Deeper and deeper.

The old man then gently took the boy's face in his hands, turned it towards his own and blew into the boy's mouth . . .

The boy felt as if all the stars and galaxies in the universe were being blown right into his being. Blown straight into him . . . Swirling and expanding in him . . . And then coming to rest . . . in the *exact* location that they occupied in the heavens. All the stars in the heavens . . . right here inside of him. Then, in the next instant, he was standing in the center of an immense glass globe that was filled with stars, and had just been vigorously shaken.

Millions . . . *billions* of stars began whirling down around him . . . Softly alighting on his head . . . piling up on his shoulders . . . catching in his hair . . . Twinkling . . . Sparkling . . .

Just before the boy lost consciousness of his self . . .of his *former* self . . . of what he *once* was . . . he heard the fading voice of the old bluesman.

"Wait, Son!" said the voice, "I almost forgot! That man give me this too. An' you gonna need it, boy. All bluesmen need a '*Hand*'". This here's ol' John the Conqueror. He'll look out for ya, Son. But remember: Don't *never* let no one touch him. It'll break the spell if ya do . . . An' don't *never* let him outta his pouch. 'Cause, if ya do, he'll run off an' go help somebody else . . . "

As the voice paled to faint whisper and was whisked away by the wind, the boy felt the *Mojo Hand* being placed around his neck . . . Then everything went blank.

When the boy awoke he was sitting in front of the juke joint behind the wheel of his truck. The sun was shining bright and he could feel the Delta heat beginning to rise up from the earth. He looked around, but the old man was nowhere to be seen. Unconsciously he fingered the small black pouch that hung lightly around his neck.

"Come on, man, what're we waitin' for." A voice said.

He turned, and there was his friend – staring at him through the cab window. The boy stared at him for a moment, trying to collect his thoughts.

"What time is it?" He asked, still a bit fuzzy in the head. "How long we been sittin' out here?"

His friend glanced at his watch. "It's nine O'clock. An' I found you sleepin' out here about three hours ago."

"Where's the old man," the boy asked

"What old man?" his friend answered.

"The one that was playin' blues here last night."

"How do I know. Musta went home, or somethin'".

His friend opened the door of the truck and jumped in beside him. "Come on, man let's go," he said. "I'm gettin' hungry."

"Did you . . . catch his name?" the boy inquired.

"Who's name?" his friend answered.

"The old man's."

"How would I know his name, man?" his friend said impatiently. "Come on. Let's get outta here. It's gonna start gettin' real hot around here soon."

The boy stared out of the windshield and up into the bright, morning sky. Three doves whisked across the cotton fields – appearing to fly straight into the rising sun. As he watched them sweep by he tried to sort out in his mind all that had occurred last night . . . *"Did it happen?"*

Far off in the distance he could hear singing coming from one of the small country churches somewhere in the area . . .

"He's my light, He's my shield
He's my strength when I'm in the field.
Makes no difference what you may say,
I'm goin' down on my knees an' pray
I'm gonna wait . . . Wait on Jesus
Until He comes."

"It's Sunday morning," he thought to himself, and smiled.

The boy raised his arms, stretched loudly and scratched his head. Then he shrugged, pulled out his pack of Pall Malls, lit one, and proceeded to crank up the truck's slumbering engine. The engine caught with a loud bang. The truck heaved forward, bouncing and jarring, as it made its way back to the main road. Then the boy pressed down hard on the gas and the truck lurched away in a cloud of choking Delta dust.

Well, what happened that night *happened* . . . There's no way it can be proven, but it did.

The boy started playing the blues soon after that – *good* blues – and he's been playing them ever since. It can't be known how long he'll go on playing . . . but it'll be long enough for him to pass on what he received to someone else . . . The *right* someone else, I'm sure. Until then, he'll be on the road. Traveling from town to town, playing the blues and sharing the *Gift* with the folks that come to hear him.

≈ ≈ ≈

The spattering of rain on the windshield brings the old man back to the present and the highway. He automatically switches on the wipers. The right one was stuck . . . As usual.

"Damn blade," he mutters, "I'll get it fixed when I stop for gas."

Reaching over into the glove compartment, he pulls out the flask, pops it open and takes a long swallow. "Ahhh," he hisses loudly.

Peering up through the rain drenched windshield he spots the big green highway sign ahead:

PENNSYLVANIA 100 MILES. Behind it, the dawn sky issues its solemn report: Cold, grey, and rainy. He's about to cut off the headlights, but changes his mind and leaves them burning. He shakes a Pall Mall out of the pack, punches the lighter, lights up and takes a long, hard pull . . . allowing the grey smoke to trickle slowly out of his nose.

As he unconsciously fingers the small black pouch, which hangs lightly around his neck he begins singing softly to himself . . .

> *"Well, I dreamed I was a catfish*
> *Swimmin' in the deep blue sea,*
> *I had all you pretty woman*
> *Fishin after me . . .*
> *Oh, Well . . . Sho' 'nuf, I did*
> *Oh, Lord . . . Sho' 'nuf, I did."*

DIE RAT DIE

This story is true. I will narrate it to you as best as I can – the way it was told to me on that dreary night in the late fall of 1973 ... by one who was there ...

IT WAS ONE O'clock in the morning. I remember the time distinctly from hearing the church bell three blocks away toll. I was sitting in my usual wooden booth at the *Déjà vu,* a popular artists' café, located over on East 11th Street between Avenues A and B. I gazed glumly out of the window while idly sipping on my now tepid mug of Earl Grey. Outside the night was filled with gusting winds that whipped torn shreds of ominous grey clouds across the somber sky. I watched as it snatched, one by one, the last of summer's withered, brown leaves from the almost barren trees in Tompkins Square Park across the street.

I had come here originally to try and write something, but my mind began wandering in and out of focus and I was unable to concentrate. I finally gave it up and was just sitting there – the first two pages of my yellow legal pad filled with gibberish and doodles – staring blankly out of the window, chain-smoking Pall Malls and silently grieving the coming of winter.

As I've grown older, winter has become my enemy. The bleak, freezing days, the long, dark, bitter nights . . . All of these have become more burdensome as the years roll by. I was thinking of how, a few weeks ago, I had rejected a friend's offer to move with her to a commune in New Mexico. *"Shmuck,"* I thought to myself, remorsefully, *"You could've been sitting pretty under the warm New Mexico sun; breathing clean air and writing at your leisure. But, no. Now you're going to spend another long, cold winter in this rotten, rat infested ghetto".*

For years now, the East Village – seat of the Bohemian, Beat and Hippie generations – had been slowly declining; turning the once mellow and "quasi-artistic" community into a dangerous drug and crime infested neighborhood.

> *"Where have all the flowers gone?*
> *. . . long time passing."*

I WAS MUSING on this and other dark thoughts when the door of the café suddenly swung open and slammed back against the wall with such force that it sounded like it had just been ripped from its hinges. A harsh blast of wintery wind cut against my face driving me from my dark reverie. The door then slammed shut with a loud bang and I looked up to see what the matter was. There, standing in front of the closed door, sweating profusely and maintaining an expression of, what appeared to be stark terror, stood Buffalo. He was wearing his usual attire. An oversized, buff-grey, WWII German Luftwaffe great-coat. It was buttoned high up at the neck, with the massive collar fastened tightly around his ears – which gave his already small head a strange, 'grapefruit-like' appearance. The enormous garment hung loosely down nearly covering the tips of his worn and scuffed English riding boots. The lengthy sleeves almost completely hid his hands; exposing only the first two digits of his white, bony fingers; which seemed to be nervously attempting to writhe and twitch their way out of his fingerless, olive-drab army gloves. He wore no hat and his short, fine, dirty-blond hair had been blown almost straight up by the wind – adding to his stark appearance. His deep, irritated pink eyes were opened wide, and darted nervously back and forth across the room behind his tiny, grey-tint, Ben Franklin glasses. The tip of his chalky-white nose stuck straight out of his turned-up collar and glowed a bright, cherry-red.

Buffalo was once an exceptional air-brush artist. He was born in the South Bronx, and began his career spray painting graffiti onto the sides of subway trains when he was just a kid. When he finally got caught and was taken to court by the New York City Transit Authority, he brought his portfolio with him and showed it to the judge. The judge looked at his work and dismissed the case on the condition that Buffalo apply for a scholarship at some art school. Which he did – and was immediately accepted. In the years that followed he was commissioned by both the city and private organizations, to airbrush scenes on everything from swank office buildings, to the walls of handball courts, throughout the entire city.

His future, at one time, looked quite promising. But, like most hangers-on in the East Village, he and his talent had, over the years, deteriorated with the use – and ultimately the abuse – of drugs. He was hooked – as was I – *my real reason for not moving to New Mexico* – and hooked bad, on heroin.

His heavy boots thumped loudly across the worn,

wooden floor and over to the counter where he ordered his usual: a large steaming mug of Darjeeling. Then he turned, saw me sitting in the corner, thumped over, sat down and began staring intently out of the window as if he were waiting for someone to appear.

He sat for some time without speaking; his exposed fingertips tapping nervously against the side of his mug. He did not remove his coat, nor did he even unfasten the top button; leaving the over-large collar of the garment still turned up tightly against the tips of his bright red ears.

Finally, after some time, he slowly unbuttoned his coat, pulled a Pall Mall from my pack on the table, lit it, took a short gulp of his tea and spoke.

"How long you been here," he said – *his thoughts still seemingly dis lodged* – while staring intently out of the clouded window.

"'Bout two hours," I answered.

"Seen anybody we know?" he asked.

"Seen a few, Buff. Who're you looking for," I said.

He hesitated for a moment, then took a long drag on his cigarette and said: "Seen Greazy John?" I could feel that he was purposely averting his eyes from me.

"No. Why . . . Is he looking for me?" I said.

He didn't answer. That made me feel uncomfortable. I didn't like the thought that Greazy John might be looking for me. I didn't like Greazy John. No one liked Greazy John. Not even the guys that he grew up with over on Carmine Street in Little Italy.

John was born in a five-story, brownstone walk-up on Carmine and Bleeker Streets in the West Village. He was never really into the "Flower" movement . . . But, from his early teens on, he was *always* an addict. He was a predator; prowling the streets of the East and West Villages, preying on the weak. His one mission: Drugs – or money to buy them with.

> *"Where the jungle's creed says the strong must feed*
> *on any prey at hand*
> *I was branded a beast and I sat at the feast*
> *before I was even a man . . ."*

You would never know, when he was with you, if John had chosen *you* as his prey. That was the frightening part. He would hang with you, make money with you, cop drugs with you and use them with you. Everything would seem to be fine. Then, one day, after all the running around was done, and you were sitting down getting ready to tie up, with the stuff on the table, he would get that strange *Mad-Doctor-With-A-Sharp-Scalpel* look in his eyes, demand all the drugs and money, get up, and, if you were lucky, just walk away. I have also seen him at his worst. I have witnessed him torture someone by tying them to a chair and jabbing them with a hot ice pick, and then nipping at their body with a needle-nose pliers that had been heated cherry-red on a gas stove. Greazy John seemed to enjoy indulging in that type of depravity. He was, in my opinion – and for all intents and purposes – a *very* dangerous individual.

BUFFALO AND I sat there without talking for a long time . . . Sipping tea, smoking and staring out the window . . . our thoughts lost and drifting along with the blustering winds outside. Finally, he said, eyes still averted: "Got anything?"

"Yeah," I answered. "Back at my pad."

"Turn me on?" He asked.

I looked over at him. Sweat was now running down the side of his left temple, and drops of it were slowly dripping from his ear lobe, down into his neck. He didn't bother to wipe them away. He knew that I wouldn't say no to him. We'd both been around too long.

"You sick? . . . What happened?" I inquired, still wanting to know what it was that had caused him such severe unease.

"I'll tell you when we get to your place," he said. "Can't talk about it here. Somebody might be listenin'."

I turned and looked around the place. There were only two other people there: women that neither of us knew . . . And they were sitting way in the back facing the other way.

"Okay," I said. "C'mon."

We stood up and shuffled our way out of the booth. I picked up the Pall Malls, lighter, my two pencils, and dumped them all into my shirt pocket. I pulled my navy pea-coat from the hook on the wall, got into it and buttoned it all the way up. I took my gloves and watch cap out of my pocket, slipped them on, tucked my writing tablet under my arm and headed for the door. As we neared the door, Buffalo grabbed my arm. "You go first," he said – his thin fingers clutching at my forearm with a force that surprised me. "Look up an' down the street. See if anybody's out there."

I undid his hand from my coat, opened the door and stared up and down 11th Street. It was too dark for me to see anything. "It's Ok," I lied. It really didn't matter to me, at that point, if someone was out there or not – I was coming down and needed to get straight. "C'mon. Let's go," I said.

We stepped outside, I pulled my collar up around my ears, and we both began walking toward my place.

MY PAD WAS five blocks away. I lived on the top floor of an old brick, six-story walk-up on Avenue B, between 5th and 6th Streets. The streets were all but deserted at that hour of night. Especially in this type of weather. Just a few pimps hanging on corners, here and there – keeping an eye on their girls. At each corner, before he stepped off the curb, Buffalo turned his head and stared hard up and down the street. I acted like I didn't see him and just kept walking.

We reached my place, turned into the doorway – which, due to the lack of lighting, was almost as dark as a cave – and started up the stairs. The building was archaic and, with each footfall, the aged, wooden steps creaked mournfully. The banisters had been loosened with use and time and felt like they were going to give way if too much pressure was placed on them. The steam had been turned on a few days ago – too high, as usual – and the heat in the stairwell became more oppressive as we ascended.

When I stopped to catch my breath on the fifth floor I could feel Buffalo's presence directly behind me. He was breathing heavily and I noticed that he was holding tightly onto the back of my pea-coat. "C'mon! . . . Let's *go!*" He whispered urgently. Even in the dark, I could feel his sense of dread.

When we reached the sixth floor landing, I pulled out my ring of keys and began the gradual process of unbolting all of the three locks that secured my scant domain: Police lock first, 'dead' lock, and then, finally, the 'common' lock that came with the door – the one that no one ever relied upon.

I pushed open the door and walked blindly into the darkened kitchen towards the table where I knew a small bedside lamp was sitting. Over my left shoulder I could see Buffalo; standing like a silhouetted apparition in the center of the opened doorway, waiting for the room to be lighted. My right hand found the base of the lamp, I pulled the glove off the other hand with my teeth, ran it up the short stem of the lamp, and clicked on the light. "Sit down," I said, as I pulled off my coat and hung it over the back of a chair. "I'll get the water and the stuff . . . And take off that fucking coat, will you?" The mere sight of him sitting there in that huge bundle of wool was making me sweat more than the climb up the stairs had.

Buff – *that's what everyone that knew him called him* – plopped himself into one of the straight-backed kitchen chairs, unbuttoned the thick wool strap that fastened his collar, took a butt out of the ashtray and lit it, as I made my way into the bedroom to the shoe box in the back of the closet where I kept my stash. I took out four 'nickel' bags and headed back into the kitchen. When I reached the kitchen, I saw that Buffalo had removed his coat and gloves and had brought a glass of water over from the sink to the table. He had also taken his 'works' out of the lining of his coat, laid them on the table, and was now fiddling with a small piece of dirty cotton – extracted from god-knows-where . . . probably his navel – that would be used as a 'strainer'.

I sat down without speaking, pulled out my 007, snapped it open, slit the tape off two of the small, cellophane bags and dumped them into the metal wine cap we were using as a 'cooker'. I added two syringes of water, dropped in the cotton, struck a match and cooked the stuff up.

ABOUT TWENTY MINUTES later an annoying itch on the tip of my nose drove me from my hallowed reverie. I slowly opened my eyes, reached for the pack of Pall Malls on the table and, while scratching my afflicted nose with one hand, lit a cigarette with the other. Buffalo was sitting across from me, hunched over the back of the chair; a cigarette clamped tightly between his thin lips . . . staring intently at the small slit at the bottom of the door that opened to the hallway.

"Turn out the light," he whispered nervously, noticing that I was moving around. *"An' light a candle."*

I was beginning to get a bit annoyed with Buff's paranoiac behavior, but did as he requested.

With the wan glow from the candle caused the mood of the room to become more somber . . . more brooding.

I stared at Buffalo through the flickering glow for awhile, and then finally said: "So, Buff . . . What's up. What happened?"

He peered into the darkness beyond the candle-light for some time . . . Then spoke. This, to the best of my recollection, is what he told me . . .

"I was hustlin' over in the West Village four days ago

when I ran into Greazy John. He was gaffin' vics over on Bleeker Street in front of that rock an' roll joint. You know, sellin' ten dollar bags of oregano an' shit like that to the weekend warriors.

"Anyway, we hooked up an' started workin' both sides of the street. We were there about an hour when I hear John whistle. I look over an' see him standin' there next to some mark. He's wavin' for me to come over. As I'm crossin' the street I can make the mark out. He's a regular. Name is Panama. Not from the neighborhood but he comes around a lot.

"I step up on the curb where him an' John are standin'. John is lookin' at Panama; smilin' an' shakin' his head *yes*, while he's lightin' a cigarette that Panama just gave him. I stop in front of them an' look; first at Panama an' then at John. John's eyes seem to get smaller an' all *hooded* like . . . An' tiny sparks seem to be flickerin' right in the center of 'em too. I felt myself shudder, man. *'Maybe I'm gettin' sick,'* I think to myself . . . I shoulda' known better.

"'Buff, this is Panama,' John says. 'Panama, Buffalo.'

"'What's up,' I say, an' bum a cigarette from him without really lookin' at his face.

"While Panama is pullin' out the cigs, Greazy John says to me: 'Panama got a box of Bambitas [*liquid methamphetamine*]. Thirty vials. He wants to cop a bundle of *H*. Says he'll turn us on. Who got somethin' good?'

"All the while he's lookin' at me with those *half-closed-poison-snake* eyes of his. I hesitate for a second – wonderin' what his real plans are – then say:

92

'Jimmy Greenleaf over on 11th Street got somethin' nice.'

"Greazy John looks over at Panama. Panama shakes his head *Ok*. Then John turns an' slowly looks over at me. I can't shake that *look* in his eyes. Somethin' inside me is sayin', *'Split, Man!' Now!'* But, I say, 'Ok, let's go,' instead.

"We catch a gypsy cab – knowin' that only a *gyp*'ll wait around in that neighborhood – an' shoot over to Greenleaf's place to cop. Then we jet over to a vacant pad I know, over on 3rd an' D. While Panama is payin' the gyp I look over at John.

"'What's up,' I say, starin' straight into his eyes without lookin' away – which, let me tell you, was no easy trick. 'You lookin' to stiff this dude, or what? Let me know now, man.'

"John stares at me for a long while, an' then says, in a low voice so Panama can't hear, 'What're you a fuckin' asshole, or somethin'? Just shut the fuck up an' do the right thing, Ok?' Then he turns to Panama, smiles, an' says: 'Everything cool, man?' Panama nods his head an' we head into the building an' up four flights to the vacant pad . . . All the while I feel like I'm slippin' deeper an' deeper into darkness.

"The door to the crib is locked, but I know how to open it by slippin' my Medicaid card between the door an' the frame. It only takes a second an' we're in. The place still got lights – I got a box of Plummer's candles stashed, just in case – an' there's runnin' water, so we're pretty well set straight.

"Me an' John sit down at the table an' start to set things up – two sets of works, a spoon, cotton, an a glass of water – while Panama opens the bags an' pops the vials. We're usin' the Bams to dilute the smack – you know, a *speedball*. The tap water is only to clean the works with.

"John gets off first – as usual. Panama goes next, an' then, me. Soon as Greazy John feels the rush he gets up an' starts walkin' around through the other rooms in the dark, while me an' Panama smoke cigs, nod an' shoot the shit."

Buffalo suddenly pauses and turns his head toward the door. He tenses and listens hard. Then he seems to relax. He reaches over, pulls out a Pall Mall, lights it off the candle, takes a deep drag, lets it dribble out of his nostrils and continues.

"This same scene goes on for two days an' nights – the three of us speedballin', Greazy John gettin' off first an' goin' off somewhere in the dark, an' me an' Panama chattin' an' noddin' – with each of us takin' turns, every once in a while, to run down to the Bodega over on D for cigarettes, food, an' et cetera – all on Panama's tab, of course. I'm also makin' the run back an' fourth to Greenleaf's place on 11th Street.

"Everything was runnin' cool, man . . . Cool, that is, up until last night."

When I asked Buffalo what had happened he just sat there and stared at me for a long time. Then he took another tug off his cig and went on.

"Well . . . last night Greazy John starts actin' a bit funny . . . *Weird* is the real word. He won't talk to anyone, an' he's spendin' more an' more time wanderin' around in the other rooms in the dark. He's also startin' to spend a lot of time starin' at Panama. Somethin' that's makin' me an' Panama *very* uneasy.

"On the fourth night – tonight, now – John really starts actin' off the wall. He starts talkin' out loud to himself in the other room. I can't make out exactly what he's sayin', but I sure don't like the tone of it. All of a sudden he stomps into the room, glares at Panama with a severely neurotic look in his eye, an' starts accusin' him of bein' a *"rat"*.

" 'You're a snitch,' he says, pointin' his big, fat finger right in Panama's face. 'You're a fuckin' *rat,* man.'

"I can see Panama's face in the candlelight. It's all slick an' beaded with sweat. His lips are drawn back tight against his bony cheeks an' his eyes are glassy an' popped wide open. His hair looks *oil-soaked* an' is matted to the top of his head, an' hangin' wet an' heavy down on his skinny little shoulders.

"I'm scared too, man. I know it's mostly from all that speed an' horse we been doin', but that don't make no difference. I also know Greazy John. And I know how crazy he can get if he wants to . . . I seen him in action.

"Even though I'm startin' to feel in a near-panic-mode myself I pull it together an' say: 'Chill out, Johnny. Panama's been turnin' us on for days now. You don't have to talk to him like that.'

But what I said to him did in no way alleviate my feelin' of what might happen if John was to cut loose in that apartment.

" 'Shut the fuck up!' John barks, turnin' to me. 'An' don't *never* call me Johnny again . . . You ain't my mother . . . shithead.' he adds.

"I look up at him an' I can see that, while he's *lookin' an' talkin'* at me, his thoughts are still centered on Panama. His face is all greasy an' shinin' like a balloon. The sweat is literally *leapin'* off his forehead. His shirt is soppin' wet, unbuttoned an' opened all the way down to his waist. It's hangin' onto his shoulders like wet, brown wrappin' paper clingin' to pieces of raw meat in a butcher shop. I can almost see that jailhouse tattoo he got put on his chest when he done them five years upstate. You musta' seen it, man. It's a big, ugly *skull-an-crossbones* piece. The skull is wearin' one of them old-time, striped, brimless prison caps, cocked, 'acey-deucy', on one side of its bony head, an' it's leerin' at you with only a half a mouth of broken, an' split teeth. The crossbones under the skull's chin are all wrapped in locks an' chains. Circlin' the tat are the words: *'When this prisoner dies, send his soul to Heaven . . . He already done his time in Hell.'* A nice piece, man . . . But somethin' that, at that particular moment, I was not really *yearnin'* to look at.

"Anyway, I try to break the atmosphere by sayin', 'C'mon, man, let's cut all this bullshit an' do up some more of this stuff. I feel like I'm comin' down. What about you guys?'

"The scam seems to work. The starin' match between John an' Panama breaks up when I mention the dope, an' we start gettin' down to business again.

"John gets off first an' starts wipin' his grimy face with some filthy rag that he found in one of the other rooms somewhere. Then he takes one of the cigs off the table, lights it up an' starts starin' straight at the wall in front of him. I notice that, while he's lightin' up, his hands are shakin' a little. I'm thinkin' that maybe he overamped or somethin'. But then, as I'm watchin' him, he turns an' looks at me in the most queerest way an' says: 'You know, Buff, you're right. You are absolutely right, man. I'm sorry for talkin' like that to Panama. I guess I just been up a little too long . . . Know what I mean?' *But, all the while his eyes are shootin' sparks right at me.*

"Then John starts to turn toward Panama. Now, maybe I'm up too long also – an' startin' to lose it a little too – but I *swear* that he's turnin' his head extra slow – like in a slow-motion horror flick – an' all the while his snaky eyes are glued on mine while his head is turnin' . . . An' his lips seem to be tryin' to hold back a real profane lookin' *'Watch-this'* smile.

"Anyway, he turns to Panama an' says, 'Listen, man, I'm real sorry, Ok? I just been up too long, Ok?'

"Panama nods his head *Ok,* but I can tell by lookin' at him, that he really *ain't* Ok. He's scared shitless . . . An' it ain't from the fact that he's all fucked up on speedball – an' been like that for days now – either. He's scared of Greazy John . . . *Real* scared. I can tell . . . An' so can Greazy John.

"Well, anyway, John seems to cool down an' he's actin' like nothin' ever happened. But I can still feel the tension windin' itself all around through the room. An' I can almost taste the metal in the air on the tip of my tongue. But I don't say nothin'. I really wanna get up an' leave . . . but I know there's still some dope left, so I just sit there, waitin' to get turned on again. It was a dumb thing to do, under the circumstances, man . . . but you know how it goes, man . . . I got a *real* bad habit.

"About an hour later we start doin' up the last of the stuff. I look up an' out the window, an it's all pitch black an' evil lookin' outside. It's like a bad omen . . . Like somethin' *ghoulish* is gettin' ready to squirm in over the sill an' cover us all up.

"Panama's off somewhere, now, takin' a piss, an' me an' John are sittin' at the table gettin' ready to set it all up. For no reason John reaches up, pulls the light-chain an' switches off the light. Then, in the dark, I hear him fumblin' with the box of candles on the table. He lights a match, holds a candle that he fished outta the box to it, lights it, drips a few drops of wax on the table an' sets the candle on it. When I ask him why he wants to use a candle he says that the bright light is 'hurtin' his eyes'. He opens the last five bags an' dumps them in the cooker, cracks open the last two vials an' pours them in too. Then – *an' now I don't know if I'm trippin' or not, but* – I think I see him slip somethin' out of his shirt pocket an' pour it into the cooker with the rest of the stuff. I try to catch his attention but he acts like he's busy cookin' up an' makes like I ain't there

"Then, real quick, he calls Panama. 'Hey Panama!' he says. 'C'mon! It's your stuff, man; you get off first this time, Ok?'

"Panama walks in, looks at the candle an' then at me, an' then sits down without sayin' a word. John draws up a real big shot, takes Panama's arm an' ties it off real tight with the belt. Panama looks like he's in a pure panic now. I can see it plainly. His whole body is as stiff as a board. He wants to say somethin', but he can't, 'cause he's too scared.

"John takes the needle an' sticks him hard in the pit;

causin' Panama to jump from the pain. He fools around 'till he gets a hit, an' then he pulls off the belt an' runs the stuff right in without even waitin' to see if it's too much. In a second Panama's whole body jerks backwards an' he starts chokin' an' gaggin'. John's got him by the arm an' he starts yellin, 'I know you, motherfucker! I *know* you! You ain't nothin' but a fuckin' *rat!* You ratted out me an' Biff two years ago, an' Biff got time an' died of a heart attack while he was still in the joint. An' now it's time for *you* to die, motherfucker!' John screams at the top of his lungs. I jump up an try to grab his arm, but he won't let loose of Panama. Then he grabs me with his other hand an' pulls me close to his sweaty face. 'Look, Buff!' he yells. '*Look* at the rat's face!'

"I turn an' look at Panama. At first, through the candle-light, he looks like he's just sweatin' real bad. But then, as I look closer, I can see what's really happenin'. His skin is actually *meltin'* right in front of me! It's just *layin' open*, an' body fluid an' bright red blood is oozin' out of him all down his face an' neck. He wants to scream to me to help him. I can tell by the look on his face. But he can't. He's just starin' straight at me with his mouth wide open, an' all full of this *pink foam.*

"I try to break loose from John's grip, screamin, 'Are you fuckin' *crazy*, man!?' But he don't even hear me. He's just starin' at Panama an' laughin'. 'That's right!' he screams. 'I gave you a hot-shot, *rat!* Liquid Drano an' rat poison, man! I made it up special for you the last time I went down to the Bodega. Now I'm gonna sit right here an' watch you *die*, you fuckin' rat!'

"That crazy sonofabitch musta brought one of them

empty Bam vials down to the store with him, filled it up with that shit, sealed it up somehow an' then snuck it back up to the crib.

"An' then John starts screamin', *'Die, Rat!* . . . *Die!'* again an' again, an' over an' over. An' all the while, he's laughin' like a fuckin' insane lunatic. It was horrible, man . . . *Horrible!*

"I pull myself loose an' run out the door, an' down the stairs into the street. I was so fuckin' scared, man, that I ran all the way to Houston Street an' caught the F train up to the 'Duce' an' got lost in the crowd up in Times Square . . . Just in case that crazy motherfucker was followin' me, or somethin'.

"When I couldn't stand it no more up there – walkin' around with all those blue-coats starin' at me – I came back down here. That's when I seen you at the Déjà vu.

"What am I gonna do, man? What the *fuck* am I gonna do? I know if that insane motherfucker finds me, he's gonna kill me too! Oh, *Christ!,* man. What am I gonna do now!"

BUFFALO SAT THERE at the table for a long time; holding his head in his hands and sobbing like a baby. I really didn't know how to take what he had just told me. Was his story true? Or had he become so paranoid from shooting heroin and methamphetamine for four days that he had totally lost contact with reality.

Finally Buffalo began to regain his composure and calmed down a bit. We did up the other two bags of heroin and just sat there in silence for a long time.

"Are you sure that's what happened, Buff?" I finally

asked, not really knowing what else to say.

"I'm *sure,* man," he said. "I seen it with my own two eyes!"

Then he broke down again, sobbing, "Oh, God! I can't believe it! I can't believe it really happened!" as the scene played itself over again in his mind.

"Listen, Buff, maybe you just overamped, or something," I said, trying to console him. "Tomorrow we'll both go back to the pad and see what really happened, Ok?"

"I ain't *never* goin' back to that pad!" he shouted. *"Never!"*

BUFFALO STAYED AT my place all that night. The next morning he left and I never saw him again. About a month later someone told me that he had gone off to live in some commune in Northern California with a busload of Hippies. I find it hard to believe that he would just up and leave New York. Like he said: he had a *"real* bad habit".

Two weeks after the night that Buffalo told me what he had seen, Panama's body – or what was left of it – was accidentally discovered when a blue-coat, chasing a kid that had snatched some old Jewish woman's purse, ran into that building on 3rd Street. I heard about it on the streets . . . It never even made the papers. When I asked around what the cause of death was, "O.D." was the only reply. I asked one of the neighborhood kids, who was supposed to have been there when the coroner had the body taken away, if he had seen or heard anything else . . . Anything . . . *funny.* He just shrugged and said: "Yo, man, that cat was so ate up by rats an' roaches, man, you couldn't tell *nothin'*, man. All he look like when they found him, man, was just a big ol' piece a chop meat, yo."

I was never able to find any evidence that could either prove or disprove, to my satisfaction, what Buffalo had told me regarding the fate of Panama. Either his story was, in fact, true . . . *or* his perception had been severely distorted by the amount of drugs that he had used during those four days.

≈ ≈ ≈

That winter Greazy John froze to death in the back of an empty meat trailer over on 10th Avenue. I heard on the streets that his body was found in a half-crouched position with a hypodermic syringe sticking out of the pit of his right arm. They said that the syringe was full of blood, and that the blood had frozen solid.

"Where addicts prowl, with a tiger's growl
In search of that lethal blow
And winos crump, from that canned-heat 'brump'
You'll find their graves in the snow . . ."

BUTCH

This story is about a guy named Butch. I met Butch in nineteen sixty-seven down in the sunny state of Florida. Well, I didn't exactly *meet* him . . . *officially* meet him, so to speak . . . He was one of my cell mates in state prison.

Yes, I was down in the sunny state of Florida at that time . . . Florida state prison, that is, serving a two-year stretch for "Excessive Purchase of Opium". Now, I know when you hear a statement like "Excessive Purchase of Opium" it's easy to picture some shadowy guy, dressed in a London Fog and floppy brimmed hat, creeping around some murky waterfront, with a black leather attaché case crammed with blocks of "Golden Dragon" opium. But it's not what you think. No. The truth of the matter was that I was arrested for purchasing three one ounce bottles of Paregoric within a forty-eight hour period – which, I now know – is illegal in Florida.

Paregoric, or "PG", as it's called on the streets, is an over-the-counter medication that contains a small amount of anhydrous opium and is basically used for stomach cramps, colic, teething and the like. I can't say that I used Paregoric for any of those maladies, but I didn't think that what I was doing was such a serious offense. I had a steady job at the time, was renting a small cottage in Coconut Grove, and was driving a classy late-model Jag. I paid all my bills, owed no one anything . . . and was purchasing –

no prescription needed, and for my own personal use – an over-the-counter product which, for all intents and purposes, was just about as legitimate, in my humble opinion, as Kaopectate. Apparently the legal system in Florida was not in agreement with me. I was arrested, taken into custody, convicted, and sentenced to two years hard labor. I was held over at Dade County Jail for approximately two weeks, and then driven in the Black Mariah to Raiford prison; a facility located near the small town of Stark.

Raiford prison was one of the oldest structures still standing in the Florida state prison system at the time. It was built from coral rock, cold-rolled steel and convict's sweat. The entire compound housed approximately one thousand men. At that time the Florida state prison system was still segregated. Five hundred Blacks lived on the east side of the complex, and five hundred whites lived on the west side.

Raiford was an old prison. A *very* old prison. There were no tiers, as one might see in the classic "big house" movies. The unit that housed the prisoners was two stories high and consisted of winding, black, steel staircases and long, stone hallways that lead to the cells. The cells themselves had no view of the outside and had to be unlocked and locked by hand.

The cells were small in comparison to the amount of people living in them. Two-man cells were located on the first and second floors. They were once *three* man cells – that is, a one man *sized* cell, approximately 8 ½ x 11 feet, but with a triple-decker bunk in it – but the Feds visited Raiford in the early 60's, took a look at the situation, and put an end to that. Quick.

The ground floor, or "Skid Row" as it was affectionately nicknamed by the cons, was comprised of eight man cells. All new inmates, or 'fish', to use the proper prison vernacular, were sent to Skid Row upon admission. Unless, that is, you knew someone in the cells upstairs . . . or you had a lot of money. Then you went straight up to a two man cell. I didn't have a lot of money . . . and didn't really know anyone . . . I was billeted in Skid Row

The cells on Skid Row were approximately fifteen feet by twenty feet. They had no bars per se – that is, running from floor to ceiling – like in the movies – but somewhat resembled a row of low, stone cottages built one-against-the-other. Each 'cottage' had a small door in the center – two feet by five feet – and a window – three feet by four feet – on each side. The door and windows were not, however, made of wood and glass. They were built of closely arranged steel bars. The living quarters at the 'Rock', then (*another convict nickname*), resembled more an old military stockade than the conventional prisons seen in magazines and on TV.

Each cell on Skid Row was furnished with four double-decker bunks – two on the side walls and two up front against the barred windows. There was one table and one chair. In the center of the back wall was a combination sink and toilet. It had no lid and was completely made of Stainless steel. The walls of the cells were at least one and a half feet thick.

Lock-down at the Rock was 5:30 PM. Everyone had to be in their cells by then. The 'turn-key', a doddering old man of at least 60 years, would come shuffling down the hall, take count of all the prisoners on the 'Row' – locking each cell by hand as he passed, with a large, ancient looking brass key that appeared old enough to have been used at the time of Christ. At the end of the hall was a solid steel door with a small peep-hole cut into it with an acetylene torch. I imagine the peep-hole was to be used by the "screws" to safely observe us cons in case of a riot, or something. When the turn-key got to that solid steel door at the end of the hall, he locked that one too. And from then on, we were 'on our own', so to speak. For, until five-thirty the next morning – lock-out – you wouldn't see hide nor hair of any 'freeman'.

As soon as the steel door at the end of the hall was secured things would begin to relax and the 'night life' on Skid Row would begin. In our cell the big event of the evening was the ever popular – and perpetual – game of Domino. The game was never ending. It was always a work in progress. That is, at lights-out, all the dominos, or "bones" were carefully left in the exact positions on the table that they had been laid on the last play. The next evening the game would just pick up where it had left off the night before. It just went on and on like that, night after night; and, I imagine, year after year, for some of those guys.

The game they played went like this. It was called "count". It's too complicated for me to explain at this time, but basically it meant that you would count points off the exposed ends of the dominos laid on the table. The points could only be utilized if they totaled up by fives – five, ten, fifteen, and so on. The con with the highest score at the end of each hand received a two-fold prize. Cigarettes, of course were the main proceeds – Pall Malls were the thing at that time . . . no "rollees" were allowed in the game – and also the distinct honor of sitting in the only chair in the cell. The guy with the next highest score got to sit on the steel toilet – which was covered with a heavy chess board – and the third and fourth runners-up just had to stand.

So, basically, that was life on Skid Row. If you didn't play Domino, which I didn't . . . I couldn't afford "tailor-made" cigarettes . . . you just crawled up into your bunk *(being a new fish, I naturally slept on a top bunk)*, and either read a book (if you *could* read, that is . . . some of the cons there couldn't), or just laid there staring at the ceiling, sweating and swatting mosquitoes until 10: PM when the lights were turned off. You couldn't walk around in the cell . . . There just wasn't enough room. And – God Forbid! – if you had to relieve yourself before ten O'clock. You'd have to walk up to the guy that was sitting on the chessboard on top on the toilet bowl and, as politely as you could, ask him if you could use the toilet. This would invariably start a chain reaction that could become very uncomfortable – if not down right *dangerous* for you – depending on the mood of the players at the time. The con sitting on the toilet would have to get up. And that would interrupt the flow of the Domino game. And that would cause a slight case of pandemonium amongst the players to break loose. All the cons playing Domino would immediately begin bitching and cursing at you, while staring contemptibly at your pecker; yelling things like, "Hurry up, Goddammit, an' piss! . . . fer Chrissake!" I don't think I need to explain to anyone how hard it is to "piss" under that kind of pressure. Suffice to say that all use of the toilet was performed *before* the start of the Game . . . or discreetly held until lights-out.

Well, like I said before, this was the routine on Skid Row. This was all we had to look forward to . . . This was how we wiled away the evenings at Raiford. The same stale act. Night after night, and year after year. In order to survive in Raiford, you had to get used to this routine . . . And I use *"used to it"* very loosely – and for total lack of a better description. It's like saying one must get used to a bad case of hemorrhoids, or something.

But one night that routine was broken . . . By Butch.

Butch was true to his moniker. He was a big, unruly looking, brute. He wore his hair short and in a "flat-top." One of his front teeth was missing – and he had a tattoo on his right shoulder of, what appeared to be, the head of a rabid bulldog, sporting a World War I helmet and an nasty looking, spiked collar. The initials, "**U.S.M.C.**" were gravely emblazoned beneath.

Butch never did too much talking. He'd just saunter into the cell at around five-thirty, look around once – I guess, to make sure that he was in the right place – flop down in his bunk (the bottom one, of course), maybe cut a fart or two, open up a paperback western – a "shit-kicker", as they were called – and read until lights-out.

That is until this one particular night.

We had all rolled in from the yard at the sound of the whistle, on this particular night, got into the cell, got counted, pissed, and settled in for another big night of Domino and Country Western music – thoughtfully pumped in from the Captain's own personal radio.

The guy that slept on the top bunk where Butch slept was a little con named Tommy. He was serving two years for bad checks, I think.

Tommy weighed all of 110 pounds soaking wet. He was, for the most part, a pretty complacent chap, never bothering anyone.

As the scene opens, Tommy is lying in his bunk reading. So is Butch. So am I. The epic game of Domino is underway, the Country western is blaring through the PA – *"Will I ever see the green, green grass of home . . ."* – and everything is going along just hunky dory.

All of a sudden Butch looks up at the bottom of Tommy's mattress, slowly lays his book down, sets his two big ham-hocked feet onto the cell floor, hesitates a moment, and then says, "Hey, Tommy."

"Yeah, Butch?" Tommy answers.

"Ya know, you been on my mind all day," says Butch.

Tommy leans his head over the side of the bunk and says, "About what, Butch?"

Butch hesitates for a few seconds, cocks his head to one side like he's "Sparky," the RCA dog, listening "to his master's voice" and says, "I don't know, Tom . . . but if ya don't get offa it . . . (long pause) . . . I'm gonna kill ya."

It took a few moments for what Butch had just said to sink in. Yes, it *did* take a few moments for what Butch had just said to sink in – to *really* sink in – to the hard heads of us tough cons. But it did. Yes, it finally did. And *when* it did, the relative security of our little world slowly began to crack, shatter . . . and then, as if in slow motion, silently fall to pieces like a pane of fractured of glass.

No words were spoken . . . But each con in that cell gave every other con (except for Butch, of course) the *Eye* (If you know what I mean). We didn't exactly know how, when, or *what* kind of shit; but we knew that *some* kind of shit was about to come rolling down the pike . . . And right into our cell.

Butch stood there for a moment, just staring at Tommy Then he turned around, sat down on his bunk, laid back down, and began reading . . . as if nothing had ever happened.

The Domino players made like they were still playing Domino. The rest of us also made like we were either reading, smoking – or just staring up at the ceiling, and swatting flies. I was making like I was reading. It took me a few minutes, though, to realize that I was holding my book upside down. Every so often Butch would lay his book down on his massive chest and say, in a sing-song – raising his voice an octave with each word, "Tommy, you're on my mind again . . ." Adding, " . . . Don't make me get up, now . . ."

You wanna talk fear? Bro, the nervous sweat started wafting through that cell until the whole place smelled like a litter of skunks had just moved in under some con's bunk.

Now you've got to try to imagine this situation: We were all locked down in that cell – until five-thirty in the morning. With Butch: a very large and brutish man, who now appears to be, not only large and brutish; but also *very* crazy . . . And its only seven PM! There is absolutely *no* place we can go. There are no guards around – nor would there be until lock-out: *Ten* hours from now. They were all up in the Captain's office; all the way up on the other end of the compound – with about twenty hand-locked steel doors between us and them – chewing tobacco and spitting into a number ten can. I mean, that cell was virtually *bubblin'* with so much fear, (although none of us would dare show it) that I don't think you could've driven a *toothpick* up any one of our asses with anything less than a jack hammer! . . . And only *God* knows what horrors were running through poor Tommy's head.

Butch was truly a 'Bull' of a man. He was at *least* three-hundred pounds of big, mean, dumb . . . *country* . . . muscle. If he were to cut loose in that cell . . . when they opened it the morning . . . why, they'd have to come in there with sponges and ink blotters, just to mop up our remains.

We all went on "doing our thing", so to speak, but were like so many puppets on strings . . . Just going through the motions. Like I said, no real words were spoken that night, which could affirm any con's *true* feelings, but the tension in cell C-8 (that was our cell number) was so thick it could've been served up as home-made pea soup.

At lights-out everyone peeled down to their skivvies, gave each other the *Sneaky Eye,* and climbed into their respective bunks . . . But you know as well I . . . there would be no sleep tonight. Cigarettes (tailor-mades as well as rollees) were immediately lighted. And, behind each flaring match, a pair of prison-hardened, death-cold eyes could be seen. They were the eyes of frightened animals – Knowing that a deadly predator has been padlocked into the same cage as they were.

I knew one of the guys in the cell from the outside. We

used to hang around together when we lived in Miami. He was serving three years for forging scripts. He slept on the top bunk next to mine. The one against the wall. He'd light up a rollee and give me the *Look* . . . And then I'd light up one and give him back the *Look*. And vise versa. We both must've smoked about five packs apiece that night.

≈ ≈ ≈

Butch never actually physically assaulted Tommy; but he continued to threaten him throughout the night. For a long while he babbled on about how Tommy was still on his mind. Still "buggin'" him. Then, as the night wore on, he broke off into more and more abstract talk, until, finally, it became impossible for any of us to understand even a *word* that he was saying.

The climax came at about three or four in the morning. While still gibbering nonsense, Butch leapt up from his bunk and began pacing round and round the cell, in a circle. Then he stopped, jumped up onto the table and loudly announced that he had ". . . just met with the scientists. They said," he said, "that they will perform the operation . . . All that we need to do," he said, "is to slit our own throats."

The cell immediately became ablaze from the light of seven matches.

I'm sure that every con in that cell was thinking the same thing that I was: The party . . . in *this* world, at least . . . was now – or was soon to be – over. I was personally thinking how one feels when one is torn into small pieces like last week's betting slips. And all for just three ounces of PG!

After what seemed like two or three eternities, the

night finally passed. At four forty-five in the morning you can bet that every con in that cell had gotten dressed – in the dark – and was 'marking time' at the cell door. Every man, that is, except Butch. Butch was crouched in one of the corners, mumbling something unintelligible to himself.

When the lights came on at five, we were all lined up. Right in front of the gate; waiting for the old turn-key.

Now, like I said before, the cell doors in Raiford are *very* narrow. Only one man can fit through them at a time. You even had to duck your head in order to get through.

I guess it was made that way so that prisoners couldn't rush the guard or something.

Anyway, at precisely five-thirty, the old turnkey comes shuffling up to our cell as usual. He unlocks the gate and is about to say his usual, "Mornin', boys", when we fling open the gate and storm past him like a loaded freight train; careening down the hall at full throttle. We fly like jets through the halls, up and down the maze of stairways, and straight into the captain's office. He liked to jump clear out of his chair when we busted in.

"Hold up, Godammit!" he yelled in his southern drawl. "What the *hell's* goin' on roun' here!" (I bet he thought that we were trying to bust out or something . . . *Big ass!*)

Anyway, one of the cons hollers, "It's Butch, Sir! He done went stone crazy, or somethin', Captain! He's talkin' all outta his head!"

The Captain stared at us all for a moment. Then he sat back down, pulling a mouse-grey handkerchief out of his back pocket, and slowly mopped the sweat off his large brow. Then, while wiping the sweat from the inside of his cap, he sighs and says, "So! It's that *God*-damn Butch again. I shoulda known! Sonofabitch goes off like this every once in awhile. Don't worry, boys: He won't hurt nobody. He just wants some attention. You know . . . to be alone for awhile. We'll go pick him up an' take him over to the Psyche ward at the hospital. Then the Doc will fill him up with Thorazine and throw him in the padded cell. In a few weeks he'll be good as new. Now you boys go on to chow. He'll be gone by the time you get back."

None of us went back to the cell after chow. In fact we all stayed away from that cell until lock-up that night. When we got there we saw that Butch's mattress had been removed.

That night – even though, between us all, there was a total of eighty-seven and one half years sitting in that cell – we all slept sound as an egg – so-to-speak.

≈ ≈ ≈

Two weeks later I'm laying in my bunk reading "The Complete A to Z Guide to Astro-Projection" (or some other Escapist bullshit) when there's a knock on the wall from the cell next door to ours.

"Yeah," I say, not really paying any attention.

"Hey, boys! . . . Ha' Ya'll doin'! . . . (long pause) . . . It's me, Butch!"

One of the guys slams a bone down on the table and yells, "Domino!"

THE DOCTOR IS OUT...

Some time ago on a lazy autumn day, while aimlessly strolling through Washington Square Park, kicking up leaves and reminiscing on days long gone by, I chanced to meet an old friend whom I had played music with years ago. We had been street singers – troubadours – playing folk songs on the streets of Greenwich Village. We hadn't seen each other for years but recognized one another immediately. The day was mild and sunny and we decided to have lunch together – to update one another on our current lives and, of course, resurrect, commemorate and perpetuate the 'good ol' days'. We dined at Monty's, a small trattoria on McDougal Street. The fare was good: Fresh Caesar salad, homemade Fettuccini Alfredo and a chilled carafe of white, "Vino de Casa".

Satiated and serene, we paid our bill and casually meandered across Houston Street heading due south – ending up at a small café in SoHo we had often frequented in the past. It was the place we came to relax after troubadouring through the Village all day.

We sat al fresco – sheltered and cool under the familiar fringed, Italian striped awning – smoking cigarettes, sipping iced Espresso Lungo, idly prattling about the elusive 'goose egg' and aloofly observing the diversified mélange of humanity aimlessly drifting past our small table.

We spoke of the time when we both lived in the Hog

Farm – a somewhat 'upper echelon' Hippie commune, located on Broadway and Houston Streets during the late '60s. We spoke of the days we had spent playing music on the streets and around the fountain in Washington Square Park – standing, fully clothed, in the icy-cold spray of the fountain to cool off . . . and also to help us come down from the potent weed we had smoked. We talked of the warm summer nights spent on the roof of the Hells Angels' headquarters on East 4th Street smoking pot and star gazing with our "chicks". We would play guitars and spout gibberish till dawn – solving all the unsolvable Mysteries of the Universe. We reminisced about the days long ago when we were brave, carefree and bulletproof.

"Yes", we concluded, "those were wonderful times. Truly, a "Magical Mystery Tour." We both agreed that we missed those days. But we laughingly concurred that, although the memories of those days were precious, they were better off consigned to their present locale: stored away – lovingly and carefully in shrouded, candle-lit grottos – deep within our minds. Only to be retrieved, every now and again, in the presence of a few well-chosen chums – admired, venerated, and then carefully wrapped back up in crisp white tissue paper and replaced, safe and sound, into their shrouded repositories; to be savored once again, at a future date, like a fine wine.

We were both professionals now – had shaved our beards, bathed, cut our hair – and had even been steadily employed for years. Neither of us had any sincere desire, at this point in our lives, to spend the night on the roof of the Hells Angels' headquarters discoursing on the functions and dysfunction's of the Creator – Although, on rare occasion, I did sometimes yearn for a nice fat joint of Acapulco Gold.

As the hours passed lazily by our conversation casually turned to drugs. We had surely done our share of drugs in the Sixties. But were either of us still using at present? "No", we both affirmed, we had given them up years ago. They were "dangerous and illegal". Two things that had no place in our now ordered and regulated lives. Although I did mention during the conversation that I was having "somewhat of a problem obtaining diazepam." I didn't really consider Valium a drug – I kept it in my medicine chest for occasional sleeplessness and nervous tension. A long time physician/friend who prescribed it for me had retired and moved to Florida, and I felt a bit uneasy about going through all the trouble of making a doctor's appointment just to ask some physician that I wasn't familiar with for something like that. My friend mentioned that he knew a certain Doctor Gnotzi, who would probably prescribe the drug for me. He said that, although he hadn't been to his office in a long while, he was sure that the Doctor was still at the same location.

"A well respected man . . . Been there for years . . . Right over in the West Village," he said as wrote down the address on the back of his business card and handed it to me. "He's a real nice guy. He'll take care of you".

We lingered a bit longer at the café and then aimlessly wandered across Canal Street to Chinatown, ate a few steamed pork buns, exchanged phone numbers and said good-bye – promising to call one another soon – as we went our separate ways.

ABOUT A MONTH later I happened to be in the West Village on business and saw the building my friend had mentioned the doctor's office was located in. It was an old and respectable structure, situated on the corner of Greenwich and Christopher Streets.

I had some spare time on my hands and, assuming that I wouldn't be in the doctor's office too long, decided to stop in. I walked across the street – locating the entrance to the building on the Christopher Street side. The entrance was sheltered by a long, green canopy that extended all the way to the curb. The doors to the vestibule were made of highly polished brass and fitted with sparkly-clean French windows. A doorman, nattily attired in a crisp grey uniform, black Patent leather shoes, cap and white cotton gloves, politely opened one of the doors for me as I approached. I entered, smiled, and thanked him. He lightly tipped his cap as I passed. I stepped into the vestibule – assured by the courtly surroundings, that all would be well. Turning left I saw a shiny brass plaque with the name A. Gonzti – MD engraved on it – accompanied by an arrow, pointing to a mahogany door at the end of a carpeted hallway. I walked down the hall, opened the door, and confidently sauntered in.

THE INSIDE OF the doctor's office and the hallway I had just left were as opposing as day and night. The tranquility I had experienced, both outside the building and in the lobby, was immediately shattered by a trumpeting and roughhousing akin to the ringing in of the New Year at Times Square . . . or, perhaps more appropriately, a welfare office in the South Bronx, at 3:00 PM on Friday.

The office was crammed to bursting with a grisly collection of, what appeared to be the lowest dregs of humanity. All about the office small clots of these "patients" were sitting, standing or, generally, just milling about. They did not speak . . . but literally screamed back and forth to one other from either sides of the room. Newspapers, cigarette butts, empty and half-empty wine bottles, bits and pieces of balled-up paper and other unidentifiable matter, were strewn helter-skelter across the floor and chairs. I gazed about the office in disbelief – which bordered slightly on absolute panic – as the sea of sweaty flesh began to engulf me. I was certain that this was not the doctor's office that my friend had recommended to me. "I must've entered the wrong door," I said to myself, a bit shaken. As I raised both my arms to protect myself from the pushing and shoving wall of bodies closing in around me I shouted blindly into the fray: "Is this Doctor Gnotzi's office? . . . Is there a receptionist here?" No one answered and as I turned, preparing to leave, a clamorous voice barked from the middle of a crowd of gaggling cretins: "She's ova dere, Mac!" I turned and saw a disembodied finger sticking up from the midst of the rabble, ominously pointing down the corridor to my right. I looked towards where the finger was pointing and saw the receptionist. "She" – an extremely obese, high-yellow, transvestite – squatted regally – like the proverbial "Frog Prince (ess)" – behind a particularly tiny, Formica and chrome desk. Her thickset knees jutted bluntly over the desktop. Two Lilliputian-sized white nurses wedgies, daintily attached to massive, watermelon sized calves, peeped out from either corner of the desk. She was literally crammed into an immaculately clean, short-sleeved, white pantsuit. The sleeves of the jacket were so tight, that the flesh on her arms oozed out of the ends of them like rising dough. Her pants were so constricting they appeared to be on the very threshold of bursting to shreds if she were to, as much as, cross her legs too quickly. Her hair was dyed a blazing orange and was curled tightly to her head. She wore Shocking Pink lipstick that was meticulously applied just a 'jet' beyond her own generously proportioned lips. Her eyebrows were penciled a dark sable, began at the bridge of her nose – arching surrealistically, at right and left flanks to either temple. The entire space between her eyebrows and eyelids was shadowed a deep turquoise.

Through the chaos our eyes met. She gazed sternly at me. I felt myself stiffen.

"Wha's Yo Name!" she roared, pronouncing every single word as though it were a complete sentence in and of itself. "I'm Suga! Commea, Sweetie! An' Tell Suga Yo Name!"

I cringed involuntarily. Somewhere deep inside me the voice of impending danger rang out. I wheeled and was about to make a mad dash for the door. But, wanting the pills, and reckoning I'd only be here for a short while anyway, I turned and firmly pushed my way through the bastion of protoplasm that separated myself from her desk.

Trying my best imitation of an innocent smile I inquired, "Hi. Is Doctor Gnotzi in?"

"Wha's Yo Name, Sweetie!?" She bellowed as she fumbled about on her desk, looking for God-knows-what.

"My name is Corriano," I answered, timidly.

"Wha's Yo' Name? Co . . . Re . . . An . . . O?" She pursed her lips and quickly scribbled something on a doodle-covered pad. Then, without looking up, she hooted, "You Got A 'Pointment, Sweetie?"

"No. No, I don't have an appointment," I stuttered, trying to remain calm. "Do I need one?" (At this point I was quite ready to make an appointment, and come back at a later date . . . or maybe not ever come back at all.)

She looked at me for a moment and then began laughing loudly – her bright pink lips extending almost to her ears. (I noticed that one of her front teeth was capped with a gold star.)

"Jus' Kiddin, Sweetie!" she answered, with a booming giggle, "You Don't Need No 'Pointment At Docta Gnotzi's! Hea! Fill Out This Hea' Fo'm An' Have A Seat!" she blared, handing me a smudged, wrinkled and over-copied sheet of paper.

The "fo'm" consisted of nothing more than a page of grainy, indecipherable gibberish, requiring (I think) the patient's signature at the bottom. I signed without hesitation – wishing to hasten all unnecessary processes – and handed it back to her.

"Is there a long wait?" I inquired, staring with a slight sense of dread at the pandemonium swirling around me . . . while silently cursing my friend for not fore-warning me about what to expect here.

"A Long Wait!?" she trumpeted, "You See All These People Hea, Don'cha?" she continued, while fervently shuffling papers around on her diminutive, untidy desktop, and randomly waving a fat stubby finger nowhere in particular. "Have A Seat, Sweetie! I'll Call Ya!"

I turned and was about to find a corner of a chair to perch on when she yelled, "Hey, Sweetie! Commea! You Got Ten Dolla's? Gimme Ten Dolla's An' I'll Put Yo Folder On Top A Dis Here Pile! Then You'll Be Next . . . Right Afta Mac Dowell!"

I quickly dug into my pocket, fished out a ten-dollar bill and handed it to her. "Anything to get out of here quick," I thought; while ruefully coming to the realization that, once I had handed her the money, I had reached the 'Point of No Return', and was now, as they say, "Committed to the Caper".

She snatched the bill with a pudgy little 'Pillsbury-dough-boy' hand and quickly thrust it down into her bosom. Then she slipped my form into a manila folder and flapped it on top of a large, untidy pile of unkempt folders with one hand, while snatching up another one off the desktop in front of her with the other, and blared loudly, "Mac Do-o-owel-l-l! You Next!"

I saw a thin, disheveled man rise and, assuming it was "Mac Do-o-owel-l-l", pushed my way over toward where he had been sitting, hoping to grab his seat, but was too late. I just stood pathetically in a crowded corner, jealously watching him enter the examining room and hoping that all this lunacy would end very soon.

A moment later the door to the doctor's office was flung open and MacDowell came rushing out into the waiting room shouting, "Hey Sugar! Commear! . . . Quick!"

Suga immediately got up and rumbled briskly into the office. She reappeared in a moment; hollering louder than before (if that was at all possible), "DA . . . DOCTA . . . IS . . . OUT . . ."

"The Doctor is out!?" I echoed angrily, not believing what I had just heard, "Where the hell did he go?"

Suga yelled again; this time finishing the sentence: "DA . . . DOCTA . . . IS . . . OUT . . . OF VODKA!" She screamed. "Now, Who Wanna Go An Buy Him Some!"

She dug into her bosom, pulled out a wad of crumpled bills, picked out one that looked suspiciously like my ten-dollar bill and began waving it wildly above her head like a flag. In a flash she was mobbed. A small crowd was instantly around her; wildly jumping up and down like a litter of capering puppies, snatching for the money. "I'll go, Sugar, I'll go!" "No, Sugar, let me go!" "No, Me!" "Please, Sugar, Me?"

One of them finally snipped the money out of her hand and ran for the door. "You Know What Kind, Don'cha? Romanoff! A Fif!" she yelled, as the man shook his head in affirmation, while slamming the door behind him. "An Hurry Yo Narra Ass Right Back! Hea?" she gruffly added, hands on hips and shaking her round head from side to side. She finally turned, mumbling to herself, and stomped back to her desk.

"What's the problem," I asked, more than a little agitated. "Is the doctor still seeing patients?"

"Ain't no problem, sweetie," she answered, in a soft, feminine tone this time – which didn't quite fit her titanic countenance – while idly shuffling through some folders that were sitting in front of her. "He jus' outta vodka, thas all. Da Docta don't see no one unless he got his vodka, see? Dat boy's comin' right back wit it . . . he damn well better, too . . . an' then everything'll be fine. Jus' fine. Jus have a seat, sweetie. You up next."

In a short while the person returned with, what appeared to be, a large bottle, wrapped tightly in a brown paper bag, and passed it to Suga. She grabbed it and stormed toward the doctor's examining room, holding the bag high above her head and hissing, "Watch Out, Fool!" to anyone who got in her way.

Many long minutes later, while trying to thumb through a four year old, dog-eared copy of Golf Pro, I saw Mr. MacDowell quietly slip out of the doctor's examining room and disappear into the throng. The door then opened again and Suga popped her carrot-topped head out bellowing loudly, "Co. Re. An. O! You Next!" I leapt up and bulldozed my way through the crowd until I reached the heavily polished mahogany door where Doctor Gnotzi was presumably billeted. As I passed her on the way in, Suga winked and whispered loudly in my direction: "If The Docta Axe's If You Been Hea Befoe, Sweetie, You Tell Him Yes!" I nodded in affirmation and returned her wink; thinking to myself with some glee that, after nearly an hour of waiting, I was finally at the very threshold of encountering the ambiguous Doctor Gnotzi. I quietly opened the door and cautiously, almost reverently, stepped inside.

I ENTERED INTO, what appeared to be, the doctor's examining room, closed the door behind me, and gazed about in utter astonishment. The room was in a state of complete shambles. A virtual mountain of files was piled haphazardly – one-upon-the-other – at each corner of the doctor's desk. They leaned precariously, and appeared to be at the very point of tumbling off onto the floor (which, by the way, some already had). Papers and empty medication boxes were scattered all about the room. On a table near the door sat numerous bottles and vials of chemicals and pills – some closed, some opened – their contents scattered along the table and across the floor below. Buried behind the crest of disorder on his desk sat the Doctor . . . Doctor A. Gnotzi – MD.

He wore a wrinkled white shirt, unstylishly complimented by excessively wide, Paisley suspenders – one strap draped forlornly across a rumpled sleeve. His black, thick-rimmed, glasses were balanced precariously on the very top of his balding forehead. His pale, puffy jowls bore the classic "five O'clock shadow" of a man who hasn't been home for days. The pen in his shirt pocket had been replaced open and was now leaking – causing a large blue stain to slowly spread out onto his pocket and shirt. In front of him, among the debris, was the fifth of vodka . . . now one third empty. I slowly stared around at the chaos, mentally sifting through the disarray. I could see that underneath all this mess was, what had once been, a clean, orderly examining room. On the wall behind the doctor's desk hung a hand-painted portrait, framed in gold, of a beautiful woman wearing a low-cut velvet gown and diamond necklace. I assumed that this was the Doctor's wife. It was evident, by the apparently trivial clues I had uncovered, that the disheveled mortal sitting behind the desk in front of me had once been a very cultured and reputable physician. Perhaps that was when my friend had been here. Years ago . . . When Doctor Gnotzi was still a "real nice guy"

My mind began to piece together Doctor Gnotzi's fall

from grace into corruption.

The Doctor had once been a very prominent practitioner in the community – I mused – and had worked long and hard to build a good clientele. He had prospered for many years and all was well. Then his wife took ill with a long-suffering – and eventually terminal – disease. All of his expertise and medical knowledge could not save her life. She died in severe pain while he watched on helplessly. All his years of practicing medicine were to no avail. After her death his world slowly began to crumble. He took to drinking to ease the pain – and was most likely also prescribing medication for himself. And now here he sat amidst the rubble of his life; lost, oblivious to his surroundings and the world and around him. A depraved soul. Very sad . . . Very sad indeed.

My thoughts were shattered by the jarring sound of the vodka bottle smacking the desk and a loud, hoarse, "Ahhh!" I snapped back to reality and looked down at the Doctor. He was staring blankly at me, as if trying to focus on my features. His lips were wet and a tiny stream of spittle slowly dribbled down one side of his stubbled chin. Small stains from the splashing vodka were beginning to appear on his shirt.

He continued to observe me for a moment and then said in a gruff, authoritative, Germanic dialect, "Vot . . . iss your name!"

"Corriano." I replied, a little shaken. "Gerald Corriano."

He shuffled some of the mess around on his desk for a moment, looking for my folder, I assume, and then pressed a button on his intercom and yelled: "Nurse! Brink me Coriano's folder!" Suga appeared almost instantly, handed him the folder, and then turned, winked at me again, and left.

The doctor opened the folder and took out the single piece of paper inside; staring at it as if he was he was actually reading what it said. (The original form had been copied so many times – and the words so wobbly and grainy – that even I couldn't have made out what it said.) Nonetheless, after examining it for a moment, he cleared his throat and spoke.

"Vot do you vont," he said; this time in a slightly less dictatorial tone.

I then proceeded to tell him of my occasional sleeplessness and nervous tension: "The doctor I was seeing was prescribing diazepam for me," I explained, "but he moved to another state and a friend recommended that I see you. He said that you could help me." And then, after thinking a moment, I added, ". . . he also prescribed liquid Vitamin B12 for me." – I used it now and then during the winter months to keep from getting colds and figured that, as long as I was here, I might as well get that too.

But, before I had a chance to finish what I was saying, the doctor interrupted me; asking, somewhat soberly, despite a slight swaying motion of his head, "Haf you effer been here before, Coriano?"

Remembering what Suga had whispered to me on my way in, I calmly answered, "Yes."

The Doctor immediately slammed both fists down on his desk so hard that one of the stacks of files instantly collapsed and fell to the floor. He leapt from his chair, almost overturning the bottle of Romanoff, and proceeded to frantically chase around me the room; cornering me at last, against the examining table. With both arms raised and flailing wildly, he screamed at the top of his lungs, "L-I-A-R! . . . L-I-A-R!" His face purpled as he leered menacingly, no more than an inch from my nose. Small drops of vodka scented spittle dotted my face. His breath gave off a foul odor that was close to toxic. I was absolutely terrified. If I could've squirmed around him at that moment, I would've flown from his office, out of the building and into the street; running for dear life, never to return there again.

While frantically attempting to fend off his flailing arms, I squeaked, "Please, Doc! . . . I only said what Suga told me to say!" – immediately ratting her out.

He glared at me for a moment. I could see the pupils of his eyes dilate, as they swam limpidly in their jaundice-tinged sockets. His breath came in short, labored gasps while his face flushed almost black. For a moment I thought . . . and almost prayed . . . that he was going to pass out, so that I could make my escape. Then, suddenly, he seemed to calm down. He blinked twice quickly, as if he were hearing something – or some one – far off in the distance. Slowly he backed away from me and returned to his desk; leaning unsteadily on it with one hand. Then, making every attempt to regain some semblance of composure, he slurred, "Neffer lie to Doctor Gnotzi . . . I am here to help you."

After a moment he turned, walked around the desk and sat down heavily into his leather chair. He took another long swig of vodka, pulled his glasses down onto the bridge of his nose, and rummaged around the clutter on his desk until he found his prescription pad. Without looking up or waiting for an answer he said, "Diazepam?" and scribbled down the prescription. He tore the script from the pad, got up and handed it to me while walking back around the desk. I glanced at it and noticed that the B12 was not written down. I started to say, "Doc, where's the vita . . ." when he broke in and said, " I cannot write for Vitamin B12 in liquid form. Come over here unt I vill gif you a shot."

I turned and, to my horror, saw him standing next to the examining table with his sleeves rolled up, swaying from side to side. He appeared to be extracting a thick, banana colored, liquid from a small brown bottle with a very old-fashioned hypodermic needle. The instrument was constructed almost entirely of steel – except for a vial-like glass cylinder cradled in the barrel used to hold the liquid. It was absolutely ancient – The exact duplicate of the ones seen in the old Frankenstein movies. It had two stabilizing rings attached to both sides of the barrel for one's fingers, and one on the plunger for the thumb. The apparatus did not appear to have been autoclaved – or even wiped off – for ages.

The doctor seemed to be smiling with a sort of 'deranged glee' as he watched the thick yellow liquid slowly being sucked from the bottle into the glass tube. When the hypo was filled he turned to me and said, "Corriano! Come here! . . . Unt take down your pants!"

I felt myself grow weak as I stared, with catatonic horror, at the contents of the ancient hypodermic.

"Vitamin B-B-B12 is p-p-p-pink, Doc," I mewled . . . "Not yellow." And then, shrinking, back I sniveled, "I don't wanna . . ." But before I could finish my blubbering he roared, "Never qvestion doctor Gnotzi! I am here to help you! Now come here . . . Unt take down your pants!"

As I stared at the needle it seemed as though my whole life was gliding swiftly past my eyes. "That stuff could be poison . . . Or, at least make me sicker than shit," I murmured to myself. "But," I went on, "what if I refuse the shot and he takes back the script . . . "

I stared at the needle again and then at the doctor. "Vell?" he said, blankly, holding my gaze. Somewhere in the room I could here a fly buzzing about: Zzzit . . . Zzzzzzit . . . Zzit!

"Fuck!" I growled, as I marched over to the examining table where the doctor was waiting with his gadget-from-hell, resignedly unfastening my belt on the way.

I unzipped my fly, pulled down my pants and, praying silently to myself, bent over the table and tightly closed my eyes. In my mind's eye I could see the needle being held high over Doctor Gnotzi's head; glinting menacingly like a German Stuka hovering over London – ready to dive and unleash its deadly cargo. I felt my body tense. Time took on a new dimension as I awaited, terrified, for the deadly blow.

Suddenly I seemed to come to my senses; wondering just what the hell was I doing here. "Too late," I thought. "Should've thought of that before you bent over this table." It's needle time, now, sonny." But, just a split second before I imagined that the needle was to be poked into the "upper right quadrant of my buttocks", I turned and slowly opened my eyes . . . One at a time. There, behind me, stood the mad Doctor Gnotzi. His right arm still raised high in the air, delicately holding the hypodermic between his fingers. His eyes were closed and he was swaying . . . oscillating . . . from side to side. He seemed to be mumbling something, or quietly snoring – but it was too low for me to comprehend which. I stared at him for a moment – in utter disbelief. And then I knew. Doctor Gnotzi was – for all intents and purposes – fast asleep on his feet.

"This man is fucking insane!" I said out loud . . . Adding, "And also as drunk as a fucking shit-house rat!" Furthermore, I reckoned, I was just as crazy to be standing here like an idiot waiting for him to give me a shot in the ass!

I hastily snatched up my pants, without bothering to zip up my fly and recklessly ran for the door; holding up my drooping drawers with one hand, while crunching the prescription tightly in the other. I thought I could hear the rasping voice of Doctor Gnotzi behind me screaming – "Vait! You! Vait!" – as I made my flight. Once in the waiting room I swept, as one possessed, past the unruly herd of patients – bowling over anyone who got in my way. I ran frantically into the hall; sailing past the doorman at supersonic speed. He stared, dumfounded, as the backdraft of my shirttails clipped him squarely in the face. I dashed out onto the sidewalk and down Christopher Street like a mad fiend turned loose; stopping only when I reached the end of an abandoned pier on West Street and the Hudson River.

I stood, staring, trance-like, towards the New Jersey shore; taking huge gulps of river-polluted air and forcefully willing myself to regain normal breathing.

Some time passed before I began to feel more 'myself'. Finally, my breathing returned to normal, I sighed heavily. "God! What a fucking madhouse that was!" I said, as I slowly opened my clenched fist to see if it still held the script. It did. Then I turned toward West Street. A small crowd had gathered at the other end of the pier and was watching me intently – probably thinking that I had gone mad, was about to tear off the rest of my clothes and throw myself into the current. "Fuck!" I rumbled, looking down and noticing the disheveled state I was still in.

Patiently waiting until I regained the rest of my faculties, I turned and squarely faced the gawking assemblage. I then, neatly and systematically, tucked in my shirt, zipped up my fly, replaced my jacket, tightened my tie, and pushed back my disheveled hair. Then, while portraying my best rendition of "Mr. Cool", I nonchalantly strolled down the pier and past the ogling crowd as if nothing out of the ordinary had ever happened – resolutely searching for the nearest pharmacy . . . and vowing to call my friend the first chance that I got.

THE MURPHY

"Some of you guys might be surprised
At what I'm about to say
An' say, 'Who is this lame who says
he knows the game
An' where did he learn to play?' . . . "

*From "The Fall"

"**C**m'on, Boy!" Raymond said, over his shoulder at me. "Why you always laggin' behind!" I had stopped to light a cig. It didn't bother me what Raymond said. He was always yellin' about one thing or another. He was just that kind'a cat. No biggie.

I lit the cig and caught up with him. "I bet it's them *got*-damn tight shoes you wearin'," he growled. "I done tol' you bout wearin' them *got*-damn thangs," he ranted on, pointin' down at my Italian flyweights while still walkin'. "A Player got-ta cover a lotta territory, boy. You got-ta wear the right shoe if you gonna be a Player. You need to git yo'self a nice pair a bro-*gans*, boy. Can't be no Player if your feets is always hurtin'."

I looked down an' scoped Raymond's kicks. He was wearin' his usual: the cheapest, tackiest, black, high-topped basketball sneakers that he could find . . . "Felony Shoes," he called 'em.

As we walked on I heard him still grumblin' under his breath while slowly shakin' his head – his usual routine for disapproval: "Dis boy ain't *neva* gonna learn."

WE STROLLED UP Eighth Avenue headin' towards Forty-Second Street – Better known to the *Players* as the *Duce*. We had met at our usual rendezvous and hangout: the Horn & Hardart Automat on Thirty-Third and Eighth. When we reached the Duce, we would turn right, head east one block, an' then cut a left into Times Square. That's where we were gonna to work – or rather *play* – tonight.

Tonight we were gonna play the *Murphy*. The Murphy's a game played mostly on guys from out of town: Guys that come to the 'Big Apple' to see the sights . . . An' to maybe sample some of that New York City Poontang . . . *If you can follow my drift.*

Anyway, when you pin one – a 'mark', that is – an' you can *always* pin 'em: they're always wearin' them lame, brown, penny loafers – *with* the pennies in 'em, of course – an' white socks. (*like, who but a stone lame wears white socks anymore?*) Oh, yeah . . . an' they always got their heads poked up; gawking at the big buildings.

Anyway, when you pin one, you ease up on 'em an' casually hip 'em to the fact that you know where some girls are. Some *nice* girls. If they bite, you escort 'em to some pad you got picked out – one that you're used to workin' in; a place that you're hip to all the exits and entrances – that's away – but not *too* far away – from Times Square – an' then proceed to relieve 'em of all their excess bread. You know, *Bread*: Dust, Green, Ba-ka-*la*, Moo-la, Ba-*loons* . . . *Money*, baby.

So, after you cop their bread, you send 'em upstairs an' tell 'em to knock on a certain apartment door – any old 'certain' door will do – where the 'Ladies' are supposed to be waitin'. If they're lucky, no one's home . . . If not, maybe some big, fat PR mama with six kids greets 'em. Or maybe her ol' man. Or maybe, their German Shepherd dog – that don't "comprenday Inglays"? Who knows? Anyway, by the time all that goes down you're headed out the front door an' back downtown. It's simple. Piece-a-cake . . . That is, if you're a good Player.

Aside from the fact of him havin' wind in his jaws most of the time, Raymond was really a cool dude. He was a real Player. He knew all the games: Stuff, Ace, Drag, Vet, Dip, Flim-Flam, Boost. He knew 'em all. He would tell me stories about the "Ol' Days" – when playin' was a "*dig-*nified *pro*-fession" (as he put it), executed by men of sharp wit. Clever men. Men of "In-ti-*lec*-tual Vitality". His guidin' principle was that a good Player never needs to resort to violence when he plays on a mark. That's because he knows that he has the advantage over the mark. Because he knows that the mark wants to either "*ex*-ecute, or acquire", somethin' that is basically illegal. An', see, that always puts the mark at a disadvantage. Because how, unless he's been physically roughed-up, could the mark call in the police? How could he call the Bulls on us if he lost his bread while attemptin' to obtain somethin' illegitimate? No way, right?

Possessin' the artfulness to have a perfect stranger give you all his bread was the hallmark of a true Player. It's this 'finesse' that distinguishes the true Player from the common street mug.

"You see deas bums runnin' roun' here, boy?" Raymond would sometimes say to me, pointin' his finger as we passed some of the 'New-Generation' Players up on the Duce. "Deas bums here, boy, ain't even the *beginnin'* of a pimple on a real Player's *ass*."

ME AN' RAYMOND were a perfect duo. That's 'cause we were complete opposites. He was over forty. I just turned nineteen. He was black. I was white. He didn't dress hip. I did. Oh, he could've dressed cooler if he wanted to – God knows, we made enough dough. But that's the way he wanted it. His dress, and mine, were all part of the Game. For all intents and purposes, he wanted the mark – an' also the "po-*leece*" – to perceive us as complete strangers. That was the beauty of it. The thing that really made it work for us. You see, Raymond's duds – baggy pants, rumpled shirt an' funky jacket – in addition to them broke-down, tacky, basketball sneakers – were all a cover. They could make him appear, at times, like some common face-in-a-crowd. Or maybe, when we went boostin' in the garment district, like a dim-witted rack jockey. Or maybe just a bum – or wino – just hangin' out on the corner. Posin' a certain stance, Raymond could literally *melt* into just about any scene. He could be the 'someone' that you really didn't pay too much attention to when you passed him on the street. He also could be the 'someone' you might not see yourself trustin' in a deal either . . . Unless *I* was there to assure you that he *was* trustworthy, honest, an' straight-up enough – in spite of his attire – to hold your bread. *All* your bread.

That's right. *I* was the guy that you could trust. I *looked* trustworthy. I always kept my pomp, D.A. an' sideburns neat an' trimmed, an' didn't sport a 'stache'. I dressed hip, but not *too* hip: dress slacks, a sport shirt, an' usually a tan or grey windbreaker. I used to wear a cap, but Raymond said I looked too 'thuggish' in it. "Take that *got-*damn skimmer ofen your head, boy!" he told me when we first started workin' together. "Who gonna give you any money if you walkin' roun' here lookin' like a *got*-damn *pic-a-roon!*" The only thing that I had – an' refused to cut loose – even for Raymond – was my taste for kicks . . . Shoes, that is. I had a true fondness for tight, black, Italian, wing-tip, flyweights. In my book Italian flyweights are hip, cool, an' *made* for stylin' an' pro-*file*-in' . . . But, definitely, *not* for schleppin' around the City all night. An', sometimes, man, after a long night traipsin' around on the bricks, my dogs would be hurtin' so bad, I could almost *hear* 'em barkin' at me. Raymond was right about wearin' "them *got*-damn tight shoes" . . . But I would never cop to it.

YEAH, RAYMOND LOOKED like the guy that you wouldn't readily trust. And *I* looked like the guy that you would. Who would've thought that we were down together? No one – no *mark*, that is – would *ever* dig that a young white "blade" an' an old, black "ne'er-do-well" were in cahoots. Never happen. An' that's why it always went down so cool.

When we went boostin' in Midtown, we *never* got popped. Here's how a typical boost would go. Raymond would walk into, say, Bonds, on Times Square, with an empty shoppin' bag. I'd be waitin' outside – halfway up the side street – with an identical bag. Except that mine would be filled with newspapers. In full sight of the store dicks, Raymond would proceed to stuff his bag with classy, expensive shirts. Then, with the dicks diggin' his every move, he would turn an' head for the side door. As soon as he got outside he would take off up the street – with the dicks hot on his ass, of course – crash into some innocent, young white kid comin' in the opposite direction (me), yell somethin' like, "*Watch out*, fool!", bulldoze me out of the way – *while we switched bags* – then continue lumberin' down the street. The dicks would run right past me an' grab Raymond – usually just before he got to the corner. While I was calmly slidin' down into the subway, I would hear Raymond yellin' at the top of his lungs to the bewildered store dicks: "Dats right, *fool! Newspapers!* Now git yo *got*-damn hands offa me!" Endin' up with the usual, after he had drawn a small crowd – and usin' his best country-boy-from-Mississippi accent (*which actually was his place of birth*), "Why dey always tinkin' dat a black man is a teef!" They always cut him loose – they *had* to. He'd meet me down at Penn Station, we'd sell the shirts to the bogus Red Caps that worked the station an' split the bread. It *always* worked.

Another game we played was a variation of the "Flim-Flam". It went somethin' like this: We'd take a worn, twenty-dollar bill an' write a phone number – or name – on the back of the bill. Then we'd go into a supermarket through separate entrances, so no one would dig that we were together. I'd buy about fifteen dollars worth of prime meat. Then I'd go to the busiest checkout counter – staffed by a teenage girl, if I could find one. Raymond would follow me an' make sure that he was the third or fourth person in line behind me. I'd pay for the meat with the twenty – holdin' the numbered side face down – get my change an' breeze. When Raymond got to the cashier he'd place a pack of gum, or somethin' small like that, in front of her, an' hand her a dollar – a crisp, new one this time. She'd ring up the sale an' give him his change. Whereupon he would look down at the palm of his hand, in total shock – as if she had just placed a small piece of bird shit, or somethin' just as bad, into it – an' then say – *very* loudly: "Lady . . . *What* is *dis!*?" holdin' his out hand so she could see just what she had done to him. The girl would stare into his out-held hand, bewildered. "It's your change, sir," would be the usual reply. "I give you a twenty dolla bill, girl!" Raymond would say. The girl would, of course, correct him, sayin', "You gave me a *dollar* bill, sir." "*Monkeyshit!*" Raymond would retort, "I give you a twenty! You tryin' ta rob me. I wanna see the manager! *Now!*" The girl, now beginnin' to get a bit unhooked, would ring for the store manager. All the while a small crowd would be gatherin' around Raymond. When the manager showed up, Raymond would begin to put up a big fuss about how the girl was tryin' to rob him, 'cause he was "jus a po black man". "I give her a twenty!" he would bellow. "I know'd I did, cause they's my lady's phone number on it!" The manager would open the cash register, pull out the top few twenties, find the one with the number written on it, an' ask Raymond what it was. Raymond would, of course, run off the correct numbers. The manager would then give the poor cashier a stern look, apologize to Raymond, take back the change in Raymond's hand an' replace it with change of a twenty. Raymond would then traipse off – mumblin', an' in a big huff, of course – with nineteen dollars change – *an'* the gum – an' meet me downtown. Then we'd go around to restaurants we knew, sell the meat, an' divvy up the proceeds. It always worked.

WE TURNED INTO Forty-second Street, occasionally noddin' to cats we knew – other hustlers, pickpockets an' general brigands that worked the Duce – as we 'jive-stepped' our way to the end of the block. (Ya always gotta keep up your image, ya know.) When we reached the end of the block we turned left into Times Square. By now it was about eleven thirty. The place was lit up like a Christmas tree – an', as usual, crawlin' with marks. We walked over to the entrance of one of the dance palaces in the middle of the block an' stopped. It was the spot we always stopped when we were gonna to play the Murphy. It was right in the middle of the block – providin' us with a clear view up an' down the street. Raymond turned to me an' said, "Now looka here, boy. You know how dis game go, right?" I nodded my head. Then he concluded: "I'm puttin' my trust in ya, boy." I nodded my head again. Then he added, "Don't fuck nuthin' up now, hear?" as he stepped off the curb an' casually zig-zagged between the chargin' taxicabs, settlin' himself into his usual spot: right next to the statue of George M. Cohan that stood on the small island in the middle of the street.

I SMILED AFTER him as he walked off. I remembered the first time he took me up here to teach me the Murphy. He stood me right here, in front of the dance palace an' said: "Now listen, boy, dis how dis game go," as he began hippin' me to the routine. I remember I had lit a cig to get myself ready for the usual knock-down-an'-drag-out lecture that was to come. "Got-*dammit*, boy!" he roared. "I'm tryin' ta *teach* ya somthin' an' you over here smokin' a *got*-damn cigarette!" Adding, "Now take dat *got*-damn thing out your face an' pay attention!"

Like I said before, Raymond really did know all the games and how to play 'em . . . It was just that he didn't think anyone else could play 'em – like they were supposed to be played . . . Like *he* wanted 'em to be played. In Raymond's eyes no one could play the game exactly right. That is, the way Raymond had designed it to be played. I always paid attention to what he said an' played my part. An' things usually went down cool. But that never stopped Raymond from expressin' his usual rebuke – the one for which I was now waitin'. I flipped the cig onto the sidewalk an' took extra-long to snuff it out with the tip of my flyweight. *"Here it comes,"* I said to myself.

"Dis boy ain't *neva* gonna learn!" he said, turnin' and starin' at a photo of one of the dance hall babes that was tacked inside the glass display window in front of the palace – as if he was speakin' directly to her – while waggin' his head like one of them dogs you see sittin' in the rear window of some PR's street-cruiser.

"Okay, Raymond," I said as innocently as I could, while makin' out like I was intently starin' at somethin' across the street – knowin' that it would get him hot, "what's the game. Waddaya want me to do."

He glared at me. "Boy. . . ?" he said, in a low voice, " . . . Is you tryin' to work on my last nerve?" He continued his menacin' stare for a moment an' then went on. "Now," he began, "You stand here in front a dis dime-a-dance joint . .

." – *the palaces had gone up to a buck a dance long ago, but he still referred to 'em as "dime-a-dance joints"* . . . *Just as he always referred to the Horn & Hardart Automat as the "Autamatic."* ". . . You stand here in front a dis dime-a-dance joint an' ketch them marks when they come walkin' by," he said, prudently lookin' around for the po-*leece*, ". . . An' make sure they from outta town," he added.

"An' . . . just *how* am I supposed to know if they're from out of town?" I inquired. (*I could see that he was really gettin' pissed, now.*)

"*Fool!*" he bellowed. "Don't you know *nuthin'!?* All dem outta town folks is always wearin' dem brown penny-loafers – *wit* da pennies in 'em – an' white socks too. Then he added, pointin' up a the big movie marquees above our heads, "An' they always got they fool heads stickin' up at them big buildings!" Concluding with, "*God!* Dis boy gonna put us *both* in the jailhouse tonight!"

I stood for a while, coolly starin' into his face. "An'?" I said.

" 'An', my *ass!*" he growled. "Jus shut yo face an' listen, boy! He waited a minute. "*Now* . . . Like I said. You stand in front a dis here dime-a-dance joint. When you see a coupla marks comin' down the street, you stop 'em an' start talkin' to 'em."

"What am I suppose say?" I asked, as innocently as I could.

"I don't care *what* you say to 'em!" he yelled impatiently. "Ax 'em fo the time . . . Ax 'em fo a match ta light one a your *got*-damn cigarettes . . . Ax em anything you want, boy! But *stop* em!"

"Okay," I said, fightin' back a smile. "Then what."

"Now, after you get 'em stopped," he went on, "you ease up real close to 'em, so's no one else can hear – *you know how slick dem got-damn undercover po-leece is roun' here* – an then you ax 'em if they lookin' fo some girls. If they say yes, then you tell 'em that you know where some is. I'll be standin' right over there in George M. *Ko*-han Square," he said pointing to the statue of George M. Cohan. "You give me the high sign, an' then I'll walk over to the place I showed ya last night." (A place we used, over on Fifty-third, between Eight and Ninth, over in Hell's Kitchen. We knew a certain *Mama Dot* that lived there. Raymond had borrowed the front door key from her an' had a copy made.) "You keep 'em here a few minutes an' then you take dem tricks over there. I'll be waitin' inside."

"Any kinda a special sign you want?" I inquired. I was playin' with his head again. Just to watch him get upset one more time.

"Got-*dammit*, boy!" he howled, "Is you tryin' to get me riled!? Put yo finger upside yo nose! Pull on yo ear! Scratch yo *got*-damn *ass*! I don't give a good *got*-damn whatcha do. Jus gimme a high sign!"

"Okay, Okay," I said, sorry that I had pulled his chain, "Give you the high sign. Then what."

He scowled at me for a moment an' then said, "Now, when you get 'em to followin' you, ya jus keep talkin'. I don't care *what*-cha say," he said – *beatin' me to the punch this time*. "Talk about the ball game. Talk about the weather. Talk about yo *mammy* if you want! Jus' don't stop talkin' till you get 'em over to the place. Now, when you get 'em to the place, you make like you ringin' the bell.

Don't mash it for real, now," he cautioned, "I'll see your feet an' come down an' do the rest."

"Got it, boy?" He asked.

"Got it," I answered.

I CONTINUED TO smile as I watched him dodge through the traffic an' sit down in his usual spot . . . Right next to the statue of George M. "*Ko*-han". He really wasn't a bad dude. He wasn't *always* fussin' at me. Only when we were workin' . . . or *playin'*, rather.

We first hooked up about four years ago. I used to hang out on the corner in front of this greazy spoon called the Terminal Diner, over on Thirty-second an' Eighth. I had just turned fifteen. I called myself bein' a cool, young 'street desperado'. You know: blue jeans, strap tee-shirt, cap pulled over one eye – A common neighborhood "tough guy" in the makin'.

Well, anyway, one night, bored an' waitin' for some action, I happened to look into the diner. I scoped Raymond inside. I didn't know him then, but I had seen him around. I pinned that he was plannin' to make a 'Dip'. He was makin' like he was tryin' to down some beat-up, ol' alarm clock – but what he *really* was doin' was sizin' up the dudes at the counter . . . *An'* their wallets. He finally zeroed-in on his target: a big, fat trucker, whose wallet was almost as fat as him. He approached the dude holdin' the clock up in the air, then jostled into the dude's back an' dipped his wallet with the other. The guy felt the dip, jumped up, turned around, an' grabbed Raymond by the arms. In the tussle Raymond twisted the guy around so that the guy's back was facin' the door, an' yelled, "Fool! Is you *crazy*!?" while he flipped the guy's wallet out onto the sidewalk. He saw me diggin' what was goin' down an' gave me the high-sign to pick it up an' run. Which I did.

Raymond told me later that he an' the dude had gotten into some kind of a big scuffle. But, even though the wallet *was* gone, an' the guy *knew* that Raymond had copped it, he just couldn't prove it. The guy let Raymond go, but said that he was gonna call the "po-*leece*" on him. Raymond told me that's when he hooked it out of the diner . . . An', knowin' him, in a big huff too, I bet.

Anyway, when Raymond got outside he looked up the block an' saw me waitin' for him over on the corner of Ninth Avenue. "You got my wallet, boy?" he said as he approached me. He had a mean look in his eye. "Yeah, I got it," I answered, tryin' to act as tough as him. "Gimme it," he said. "Here," I said, handin' over the swag. He took it, looked inside, pulled out a wad of twenty dollar bills, stared hard at me an' said, "You take anything outta here, boy?" "No," I answered, gawping straight back at him. "You *sho*, boy?" He said, givin' me that wicked "fish-eye" of his. "You callin' me a liar?" I said, maintainin' my cool. Raymond didn't say nothin'. He just kept starin' straight at me. "What . . . Did ya *want* me to?" I said, with a half-smile. Raymond looked me up an' down for a second. Then he grinned an' said, "You all right, boy." We split the bread, became partners right then an' there . . . an' have been ever since.

I LIT A cig to clear my head an' got myself ready for the evenin's work. I turned around, an' stared at my reflection in the glass case that held the photos of the girls that worked upstairs. I pulled out my pocket comb an' ran it slowly through my hair while starin' at the photos. The photos were at least five years old. Some of 'em even looked ten. I could attest to that. I knew some of the chicks personally.

Broadway was all lit up with bright lights and loud music. Each store had different music blarin' from its entranceway. People were everywhere. Bustlin', like ants on a mound. I loved it. While still starin' at my reflection, I thought of a verse of a poem I had once heard this dude recite while I was doin' a skid-bit over on Riker's Island . . .

> *"'Twas a Saturday night, an' the Jungle was bright*
> *An' the Players was stalkin' their prey*
> *An' the code was crime, down the neon line*
> *An' the weak was doomed to pay..."* *

"*Hey*, Baby!" I heard someone say, bringin' me back from my reverie. I turned my attention from the curled an' fadin' photos an' looked around. It was a cat I knew from Thirty-fourth Street. A pickpocket. A *Dip*.

"What's happnin', Son," he said, as he strolled by me, holdin' his coat open – allowin' me a peek at the bulgin' "swag bag" he had, sewn into the lining.

"It's *your* world, Baby Bro," I answered, ". . . I'm just *passin'* through it."

He winked, I gave a small salute, an' we both returned to our business.

I pulled another cig out of the pack in my shirt pocket, lit it an' was about to return to some long forgotten daydream, when I heard Raymond's whistle. I looked over an' saw him pointin' frantically to my left. He was shakin' his head and talkin' to himself. I could dig *just* what he was sayin' too: "*Dis boy ain't neva gonna learn!*"

When I looked in the direction of his wavin' hand I saw these two dudes walkin' towards me. I looked down at their feet. Check it out, man: They both were wearin' brown penny-loafers – *with* pennies in 'em – an' white socks. I looked back up. They were both gawking up at the buildings. "*Amazing!*" I thought, rememberin' the first time Raymond had hipped me to a mark's M. O.

I waited until they got about five feet from me. Then I flipped my lit cig behind me an' stepped aimlessly out into the middle of the stroll. As they got within hearin' distance, I casually positioned myself directly in front of 'em, pulled a new cig out of my pack, smiled, an' said, as innocently as I could, "Got a light, sir?" The guy on the left looked at me for a sec, then reached into his shirt pocket, pulled out a pack of matches, an' handed to me without speakin'. ("*Damn,*" I thought to myself, as I lit my cig, "*they still use these goddamn things?*")

I lit the cig an, while still lookin' down, said softly, "You fellas lookin' for some girls?"

They turned, looked at each other for a sec, an' then back at me. One of 'em finally said, "How much?"

I cautiously glanced up an' down the street – for the po-*leece* – an' said, "Twenty dollars . . . Apiece."

They hesitated for a moment an' then stared at each other again; silently conversin' with their eyes. I thought I could detect just a *hint* of a smile on the puss of the guy on the right.

Then the one on the left said, "Okay. Where are they?"

"It's not far," I said, "Come on, I'll show you," I added, steppin' to the curb an' wavin' for them to come along – while casually pullin' on my nose: the 'high sign' for Raymond.

As we weaved our way through the heavy traffic on Broadway I could see Raymond disappearin' around the corner on the other side of the street.

Rememberin' my part of the game – *'Jus' keep talkin', boy'* – I said, "Don't worry about anything, fellas, they're real nice girls. You're gonna like these girls a lot." Then I said – *beginnin' the usual lengthy dialogue that I always used, to keep the marks' mind occupied, which covered just about everythin', an' meant absolutely nothin'* – "So. How are you guys doing? You from around here? No? Where *are* you from, then?" Connecticut? I bet it's nice there . . ." An' so on an' so on, until we reached the pad.

THE PAD WAS in the middle of the block over on Fifty-third, between Eighth an' Ninth. The same one we always use for the Murphy. It was an old brownstone. After years an' years of pavin' – and then *re*-pavin' – the City had raised some of the streets near the waterfront so high that some of the older buildings were actually lower than the sidewalks. To get into this particular place you had to step down three stairs. Five or six dented, over-loaded, garbage cans sat to one side of the door. I smelled rotten lettuce or somethin' comin' from one of 'em. Across the street a small click of Puerto Ricans were hangin' out on a warehouse loading dock under the street lamp. They were all dressed the same: Black pegged pants with thick Saddle-Stitching up the seams, two-tone, pointy shoes with "Cuban" heels, white T-shirts, an' black, silk, gang jackets. Two of 'em were beatin' on Conga drums.

I walked down the stairs an' made like I was ringin' the bell – knowin' that Raymond was standin' on the stairs inside an' would see me. After a moment he came down, opened the door an' stepped out. I noticed that he was wearin' a tan, Camelhair overcoat, an' a cream-colored Stetson hat. I wondered where he had copped them. *"Probably borrowed 'em from Happy – Mamma Dot's old man,"* I thought. The coat neatly hid his baggy pants – an' *almost* hid those beat-up felony shoes he was wearin'. . It was a nice thread. So was the crown. He looked cool. "Good evening," he said to me, in his perfect 'Player's' dialect – *it always amazed me how quickly Raymond could switch his accent an' style to fit the moment – he never missed a trick, that Raymond.* Then he looked over at the two marks an' added: "Good evening, gentleman."

"This is Tommy an' Bobby," I said, deliberately givin' them false names to make 'em feel like I was 'lookin' out for 'em' – an' also to set 'em up in the middle of a lie. "An' this is Mack," I said, pointin' to Raymond.

"Nice to meet you," he said, shakin' each of their hands. "Now what can I do for you," he said, givin' me an inquirin' look.

"These are my friends," I began – further perpetuatin' the fabrication. "They just came in from Connecticut. They're lookin' for some girls."

"You know Ralph?" he asked, turnin' to the marks, while pointin' in my direction, "I don't do business with strangers – unless someone I know recommends them to me."

They both lied yes, that they knew me.

"Well," said Raymond – beginnin' the game – testin' them now; to see how much bread they had . . . and how far they were willin' to go with it, "I have two girls up in apartment five that aren't busy. They're twenty-five dollars apiece . . . For an hour."

The two dudes look at each other – an' then at me – an' then back at Raymond.

"Ahh . . . Ralph . . . said that it was only twenty," one of the marks says.

"Well . . . The twenty is for the girls," Raymond says, "The five is a tip for Ralph," pointin' in my direction, while givin' them a vaguely malicious glance.

The hook dangled in the air . . .

"Oh . . . Right," the other one finally said.

The hook caught. An' now Raymond now proceeded to reel in the line.

I looked down at Raymond's sleeve an' dug the thin edge of a white envelope peepin' out from it. What he was plannin' – after he got the initial twenty-five from each of them – was to run part two of the game: which was that he wasn't gonna be responsible for any dough that the dudes kept with them while they were up there with the girls – "girls will be girls, you know" – unless he first counted it, put it in an envelope, sealed it, wrote the amount on it, an' initialed it. He would tell the marks that, when the girls peeped his John Henry on the envelope, they would refrain from trying anythin' "ni-*farious*" with the dough. If the marks agreed to this, he would pull an envelope out of his coat pocket, take their remaining bread, count it, put it in the envelope an' seal it up right in front of them. Then, while turnin' his back, *appearin'* to be placin' the envelope on the wall so that he could write the amount on it an' sign it, he would shove it up his sleeve an' switch it with the one he had stashed there – The one that was filled with newspapers cut to the size of dollar bills with one real one on each end – the Sham one. Then he'd write the amount on the bogus one, sign it, an' turn an' hand that one to the marks. It always worked.

Everything seems to be goin' down hunky dory, an' I'm thinkin' about how I'm gonna spend my dough. But, just as Raymond is about to run his shtick one of the dudes says, "Say, do we have to pay you *before* or *after* we get the girls?"

Raymond squints his eyes an' gives them this funny look – Like, as if one of them had just blown a big fart or something – an' then he says, like he has also been very highly insulted: *"Before*? . . . or . . . *After*?" Do you pay *After* you leave a movie? . . . Do you pay *After* you get off the subway?"

"Oh . . . Right," says the mark, after a sec. An' then, before me or Raymond have a chance to dig what's goin' down, the dude whips a black-jack out of his coat – *or something black an' heavy, LIKE a blackjack, anyway* – an' clocks me right across the top of my head.

All of a sudden the whole scene turns into fuckin' Barnum-an'-Bailey-Three-Ring-Circus. While I'm runnin' around the garbage cans, tryin' to dodge the dudes, an' screamin' *"OOOWWW!!!"*, Raymond whirls around, splits back into the building, slams the door behind him an' locks it. Knowin' that they cain't get to him, the two dudes then proceed to chase *me* around the garbage cans with the sap. While in flight, I yell, "Hey, man, what the *fuck*'re you doin', man?"

One of the dudes answers, "We just got robbed like this an hour ago, kid. Waddaya think we are . . . *Fools,* or something?"

I try to assure them – *while skatin' through stale coffee grinds, egg shells an' slimy lettuce* – that me an' Raymond are not those type of chaps – that we are on-the-level guys. But it don't seem to sink in. They appear to still have a *really* dedicated desire to want to pop me in the head a few more times with the sap.

I yell for Raymond.

Nothing.

As I'm slippin' an' slidin' around the cans I peep through the window in the front door. I can see the tips of Raymond's felony shoes stickin' out from the top of the stairs. He's wigglin' his toes inside the sneakers an' the tips of 'em are flappin' up an' down like little rubber Ubangi lips, or somethin'.

Just as the two dudes are closin' in for the kill, I look over across the street. The two PRs have stopped beatin' on the Congas, an' them, along with the rest, are all starin' over at the scene. In my best New-York-City-Puerto-Rican I holler, "*O yay! O yay! Ven A Ca! Comear, man! . . . Pronto!*"

Thinkin' that I'm a "*Compañero*", they all come racin' across the street to my aide – switch-blades drawn an' gold teeth flashin'.

"*Hey! . . . Mothafuckas!*" one of 'em yells as they reach the middle of the street. "*Wha chu thin you doin wit our fuckin bro, man!*"

The two dudes see the Ricans comin'. They quick-look at each other, the one dude drops the sap, and they both take off down the street.

The Ricans show up as I'm diggin' myself out from a pile of knocked-over garbage. "Thanks, man," I say . . . in English, this time. They all look hard at me for a minute, an' then at each other, thinking, I guess, *"Is this fuckin' dude a 'Compinche', man, or what?"* Then one of 'em – the *Hefe*, I guess – laughs. An' then everybody else laughs an' everything is cool again.

"Jo, Baby," he finally says, with a big fat grin, exposing two, gold-capped gators, "Chu almos' got chu fuckin' gringo ass kicked, *Eh?*"

I shrug my shoulders, smile an' say. "Grassyass, man."

Then, on some secret PR signal, they all turn, snap their switchblades closed, shove 'em into their back pockets, an' schlep back over to the loading platform, laughin' and babblin' in Spanish. In a minute I hear the Congas start up again.

I straighten my crumpled duds an' push back my hair, while I step out over the stale garbage an' scattered cans, wipin' soggy lettuce an' egg shells from the tips of my flyweights. Then I carefully finger the large – *an' fast growin' larger* – lump on the top of my head.

Then I turn an' stand right in front of the door. "Hey, *Raymond!*" I yell. I'm pissed that he didn't come down an' help me. *Real* pissed. "Oh . . . *Ra-a-a-y-mond?*" I yell again, scopin' the tips of his beat-up felony shoes flappin' at me from the top of the stairs. "It's okay, now . . . *Raymond*," I say, ". . . .The big, bad Boogie-dudes have split . . . You can come out now, man."

In a moment I dig the felony shoes slowly descendin' the stairs. Then Raymond's legs are showin'. An' then I can peep the Camelhair vine. Finally the door opens an' Raymond strolls nonchalantly out, up the stairs, an' onto the stroll. He stares idly over at the Ricans across the street. He don't say nothin' to me.

"Yo, man," I say. "Where the fuck *were* you, man."

Raymond slowly turns an' looks at me – *A long pause.* Then he turns an' looks back over across the street. Then he casually buttons the Camelhair overcoat, cocks the Stetson *Ace-Duce-Trey* on his head, an', while executin' a cool saunter down the sidewalk, nonchalantly says over his shoulder, "Son," – *long pause* – " . . . they ain't no sense in *both* of us gettin' our asses whupped . . . Is they? Now C'mon," he continues, wavin' his arm while still walkin', "Let's go see if we can find us two mo' marks. My rent's due tomorra."

As he walks away he slowly shakes his head. I hear him say, almost in a whisper, "Dis boy ain't *neva* gonna learn."

THE VISITOR

*M*id December. Frigid, overcast, dismal. A winter storm was moving in and outside the wind was beginning to shriek loudly. I sat in my easy chair staring at the hearth before me – studying the flames and live coals that danced and cracked around the scorched logs. I was listening to classical music. The featured composer for the evening was Wagner. Wagner's music fit the mood of this night perfectly.

On my lap lay the Bhagavad-Gita. Since I've reached my mid-life plateau, I have become more and more interested in philosophical and spiritual material. The 'Gita was one of my favorites. I opened the book to the first chapter and began to read. Sañjaya, faithful secretary to the blind king Dhrtarāstra, was describing to him the great din made by each of the opposing armies – the Kurus and the Pandus – as they gathered on either sides of the Valley of Dharma prior to the Great Battle. I had just arrived at the passage, ". . . and thereupon conchs, drums, tambours, gongs and trumpets straightaway struck up and wild was the sound that rose . . ." when, a clamorous blast of wind crashed abruptly against the house, breaking my concentration. Startled, I looked up and stared through the window into the whirling torrent outside. Huge white flakes of snow were swirling wildly about while the wind howled ferociously from tree to tree. The sound of the gusting storm *appeared vaguely familiar to me. At once – and for no apparent reason – I felt an uneasy agitation course through my body . . . along with an odd sensation of déjà vu. But from where these feelings came I could not say. Then, as the wind again hurled itself forcefully against the side of the house, I thought I could detect a single, almost inaudible, word being hauntingly whisked through the turbulent air: . . . K A T H Y . . . Wagner's morose concerto slowly faded to a vanishing point and, as my concentration became more fixed on the tempest outside, the rowdy sounds of the '60s rock group, Iron Butterfly, began to take its place – rising louder and louder until it echoed through the entire house:*

> *"In A Gadda Da Vida, Baby,*
> *Don't You Know That I'll Always Be Tru-ue . . ."*
> *And, in a wink of an eye, it all came back to me . . .*

It was the bitter cold winter of 1969. A girl named Kathy and I were living in a crumbling tenement down on the Lower East Side of Manhattan. At that time, the Lower East Side was a sprawling ghetto that tenaciously hugged the southeastern tip of the rank-smelling East River. It began somewhere around 14th Street and 2nd Avenue and rambled, zig-zagedly southward, terminating vaguely at Water Street and the FDR Drive. The Latinos that lived there pronounced it "*Loesida.*" The word rolled off the tongue easily and was soon adopted by all the denizens of that deviant domain. Hippies, artists, old Romanian and Polish Jews, musicians, bikers, working class Puerto Ricans, witches and magicians – both good *and* evil – winos, potheads, speed freaks, heroin addicts, et cetera and et cetera, all lived together in *La Loesida*. It was a bubbling vichyssoise of humanity . . . A microcosmic mural that mirrored the full spectrum of humankind.

The entire area was in a slow state of decline. Abandoned buildings dotted each block like so many black squares on a red checkerboard. Garbage was either crammed into already full-to-bursting cans . . . or just thrown down the airshafts of bathrooms. In the summer the streets reeked of dog shit.

We had an apartment in a deteriorating, five-story, brick walk-up on East 3rd Street, located between Avenues B and C. For years black soot spewing from the factories in Brooklyn and small sweatshops in the area had fused itself to the front of the building, leaving the entire façade the appearance of having been scorched by an enormous blowtorch. Most of the windows were unwashed, cracked, and carelessly patched with masking tape. The fire escape was perpetually littered with wet clothing that flapped like flags on a masthead. Boxes were stacked disorderly on every landing. Tenants clamored up and down the rotting steel rungs like ants; engaged in one sort of business or another – mostly illegal.

Our apartment was on the ground floor. It had once been a stable, which quartered two, possibly three, overworked horses that wearily hauled creaking wagons through the winding labyrinths of the crowded neighborhood at the turn of the century. However, according to the man who owned the store next to us—and who had been born in the neighborhood—the open front facing the street was bricked up about twenty years ago and the stable had been turned into an apartment. A group of Socialist/Anarchists that had lived there before us gave us the place. Furniture included. When they left they moved into an apartment right next door to the police station on East 7th Street. Don't ask me why they moved there . . . I won't tell.

Our apartment consisted of three rooms: a bedroom, a kitchen, and in the front, facing the street, a large parlor. It also included a separate bathroom. Very rare, indeed, for that area. Most apartments in that neighborhood were turn-of-the-century "room-and-a-halves", with small, enclosed water closet set off to one side of the kitchen and an old-fashioned cast-iron bathtub squatting offensively right next to the sink. Because the place was originally designed to be a stable, the ceilings were twelve feet high – as opposed to the ten feet of an average apartment. There was a barred Police lock on the door and padlocked sliding gates on all of the windows when we moved in. We were never given the keys to open the gates in case of an emergency.

AT THE TIME Kathy and I had been experimenting with a drug called D-5. Its effects were vaguely similar to methamphetamine and mescaline . . . only *much* more potent. Todd, an alchemist, occult scientist, student of "Transcendental Magick" and close friend of ours, had concocted it while experimenting with different mixtures of stimulants, psychedelics, and other rare and mysterious compounds and potions that he claimed to have acquired while traveling in the Far East. He claimed that while on a pilgrimage to the Himalayas seeking mystical enlightenment he had met a monk, a withered old creature, who claimed to have been a long-time colleague and confidant of Aleister Crowley. Crowley. The "Beast." 666. The outcast rouge of the highly questionable Occult society dubbed the Hermetic Order of the Golden Dawn that had been established in England at the end of the nineteenth century. I had read a little about Crowley and the Order, but not enough to really understand the full impact of what Todd claimed he had stumbled upon.

The monk also professed to have in his possession, not only some of the original manuscripts used by the Golden Dawn for their rituals, but also unpublished writings by an Éliphas Lévi. The man who, according to Todd, is regarded by occultists as the Ultimate Guru of Occult Science and Kabalism.

I wondered how old the monk professed to be and had asked Todd.

"He never actually told me his age," Todd answered, "But by the look of him, he appeared to be at least a hundred. He told me that, at sometime near the beginning of the Second World War – give or take a few years; he couldn't be exact – he had contrived a plan, using a 'willing participant', to make it appear as though he had 'passed on'. With his death affirmed, he then traveled, undetected – and unencumbered by his past – to the Himalayas to study Buddhism."

Todd went on.

"If he's the same person I'm thinking of, he's a man called Arthur Edward Waite. Waite, who *was*, in fact, one of Crowley's confidants, was reported to have died at just about that same time. He was very deep into the occult, magick and mysticism."

I knew nothing of the man he spoke of.

The old man told Todd that he had lengthened his life, and heightened his psychic powers, by ingesting an elixir that he produced by means of alchemy. Also by performing certain obscure, magical rites and incantations. Todd said that he was so intrigued by what he saw and heard from the monk that he stayed with him for almost two years, absorbing all the knowledge that he could. Finally, after participating in many occult ordinations, and much pleading and cajoling, the monk had reluctantly consented to give Todd the formula for the elixir.

Todd explained that producing the elixir was a painstakingly meticulous process. "One must use only the exact ingredients, incantations, talismans and magical 'tools' in order to ensure a perfect product," he stated. "The entire process – that is, to produce one cubic centimeter (cc) liquid, of the elixir – takes close to eleven days and nights." Todd also told me that, along with the formula for elixir, he had been allowed to copy some writings from unpublished manuscripts that the monk claimed were actually written by Crowley and Lévi themselves.

Todd believed that, by mixing his own chemicals and compounds with the ones given him by the old monk, and by using his "state-of-the-art" laboratory equipment, he could create an elixir that would not only be more potent, but would only take a fraction of the time to produce. This new elixir could be used by those who were not heavily involved in the study and practice of the occult sciences –

omitting all the ceremonies and magic formulas, et cetera – but with much the same results. "D-5," he told me, (that's what he said he was going to name this new potion—*why*, he never mentioned) "cuts right through all the red tape." Then he smiled and said: "You know . . . Like instant coffee . . . Instant Transcendantal Experience."

Because he recognized that Kathy and I knew almost next to nothing when it came to *real* occultism and magic, Todd had chosen us to assay this strange drug and was monitoring our reactions.

THE D-5 WAS given to us in one-cc vials. It was a thick, almost black, oily substance that had to be diluted – one drop of elixir to five cc's of water – before it could be injected into the bloodstream.

I had been injecting D-5 for almost six months and had become fairly accustomed to its effects . . . and its, sometimes alarming, if not *bizarre*, side effects. These consisted mainly of insomnia, extreme restlessness, fantastic hallucinations – *transcendental visions would be Todd's description* – and, if one was not constantly mindful that they were using a highly questionable substance . . . *true* manifestations of paranoia/schizophrenia.

One peculiar idiosyncrasy I had acquired while attempting to relieve this restlessness was an obsessive compulsion to venture out in the middle of the night and dig through trash that was left on the curb for pickup. During some of these midnight forays – and with the sense-heightening assistance of D-5 – I had unearthed some truly rare, if not downright *precious*, items.

The front room of our apartment soon overflowed with old chests, religious statues, rare books, fine paintings, authentic Indian rugs and myriad assortments of random possessions too numerous for me to name at this time. I would restore some of the items that I found – selling them to antique and curio shops around town. Other pieces, that Kathy and I truly admired, we kept on display in the room – to covet and cherish privately at our leisure.

The parlor was sealed off from the rest of the apartment by a large section of heavy crushed-velvet theater curtain I had acquired – on one of my dead-of-night jaunts – from an abandoned playhouse on 2nd Avenue. I had tailored it so that it fit snugly across the entranceway; leaving no space for anyone – except the expressly invited – to view the boundless rarities within.

As time passed, and the room began to fill with more and more curios and rarities, it began to establish a certain 'presence of its own'. It seemed, at times, to even radiate an almost *Religious Ambiance.*

Todd had once asked me if he could be allowed to perform some of his occult ceremonies there. He said that the room had the "perfect vibrations" for it.

I told him no.

IT WAS ABOUT a week or so before Christmas and Kathy and I were sitting in the front room making presents for our families. We had no money to buy them anything, so were doing the next best thing. Kathy was making pouches from a huge piece of scrap leather I had found in the trash in front of a leather shop on St. Mark's Place. I was making mittens from a large fur coat I had found sitting on top of a garbage can about two blocks from our apartment.

Todd had stopped by three days before and handed us each a vile of D-5. "One of these vials comes from a new batch that I made last night," he said. "I cut the manufacturing time down to just a few hours," he continued. "Let me know if you like it."

As he was about to leave I asked him which vial was the new one. "Don't know," he said, with a queer glint in his eye, stepping toward the door, "I put both the vials in the same coat pocket before leaving my apartment and don't know which is which." *(I wondered if he had really done this unconsciously or with premeditation . . . for "experimental" purposes.)* Then, as he opened the door to leave, he turned and said, "Merry Christmas. Maybe you'll each get something nice from Santa this year."

THE WEATHER THAT whole week had been dismal and depressing – compelling us to remain indoors most of the time. On this particular night a gusting arctic wind could clearly be heard outside our apartment – howling down the frozen Barrio streets like a mad banshee. It whipped fiercely against the windows, causing them to rattle dreadfully.

It was between four and five in the morning . . . The time of night aptly referred to as the *Hour of the Wolf*. We had been up working and injecting "*D*" for three days and nights, and things were beginning to grow a bit strange.

I felt the transformation *'coming on'* the night before . . . As one can feel the onset of a cold, or some other malady, coming on. I was lying in bed trying unsuccessfully to relax, when my Siamese cat, Shadowfax, silently leapt onto the bed, lay down next to me and gently placed her paw on the side of my neck. Her touch broke my tangled thoughts. I turned and looked down at her. She stared peacefully back. She then, slowly and rather abstrusely, closed her eyes. When she opened them again I stared deeply into them. The room began to dissolve around me and I soon became aware that I was standing in the vast, barren, sand-swept landscape of ancient Egypt. The vision took place in the Valley of the Kings. As if in a dream I stood and slowly gazed around, surveying the bleak landscape before me. In the distance I could see the three Pyramids of Giza. The entire panorama was perfectly still. Void of any sound or movement. I heard a slight sound behind me and turned to look. Reclining gracefully on a gilded couch, I beheld my Shadowfax. She appeared to me in one of her previous-life manifestations – a queen, or woman of great nobility – and was dressed in regal spender. She was serenely . . . and somewhat seductively . . . observing me. The entire vision lasted only a millisecond – although it seemed as though at least an hour had passed. That vision is still quite vivid in my memory tonight. I sometimes wonder whether it was *my* hallucination that night . . . or hers.

As I mentioned before, Kathy and I hadn't gotten any sleep for three days and nights. All that time we had been listening to WNEW-FM. During the late '60s, WNEW-FM hardly ran any commercials at all. It was a never-ending montage of Acid Rock. Cream, Pink Floyd, Sgt. Pepper, Jefferson Airplane, Steppenwolf, Ravi Shankar, and countless number of other groups, all wove their endless, unbroken strands of nonstop Psychedelic Symphonics across the airways. But, after listening to it for over seventy-two hours straight, what once was music, had now become nothing more than a raging cacophony of incessant, fragmented babble. I distinctly remember, now, the last song that was playing before finally getting up to switch off the radio. It was Iron Butterfly performing *In A Gadda Da Vida.*

The spiky glare from the electric lights was beginning to irritate Kathy's eyes. She asked me to switch them off and light some candles. Which I did. We now sat, working in silence . . . Our bodies cryptically illuminated by the flickering light of the two large, white drip-candles that sat on small elephant-foot tables at either end of the room next to our seats.

Thinking back, I cannot really say that it was *'silence'* we were experiencing. The air in the room was literally *charged* with electricity. It had a definite substance to it. You could almost *feel* it . . . slowly curling and twisting around you. Every so often, the atmosphere became so volatile that tiny sparks would ignite here and there in mid-air. Not in direct view, mind you, but far off, at the very *edge* of one's vision. All the knick-knacks perched on the tables, bookshelves and old chests in the room also appeared to be saturated with energy – and virtually poised on the brink of propulsion.

I was sitting in my chair – busy working on the mittens. Kathy sat across the room, cross-legged on a deep-red, leather divan embroidering a relative's initials onto one of the pouches.

At one point, taking a break from my work to light a cigarette, I happened to look up and notice Kathy. She was turned, facing the wall . . . Talking. She wasn't actually *talking* . . . Her lips and arms were animated, giving one the *impression* that she was engaged in conversation . . . but there was no sound coming from her mouth. She turned, noticed me staring at her and immediately returned to her work. For a moment I thought to myself, *"Did I just see her talking to the wall? Or was it just . . . "* It was becoming increasingly difficult for me to define what *was* or *wasn't* real.

"Kathy, are you okay?" I inquired, a bit bewildered at what I had just witnessed.

"Yes," was her reply.

"What were you just doing?" I asked.

"Nothing," she answered, coolly.

"Just my imagination," I thought. I shrugged and went back to the mittens.

Approximately twenty minutes later I happened to look up and, once again, saw Kathy talking to the wall. She looked over, noticed me staring, and immediately acted in the same manner she had done before. This time I knew I wasn't imagining things.

"Kathy?" I said, again.

"Yes?" she answered, as if nothing at all had happened.

"What . . . were you just doing?" I said, a bit more self-assured this time of what I had seen.

"Nothing."

"I just saw you talking to the wall," I said flatly. "What were you doing?"

"You won't believe me if I tell you," she answered somewhat contritely–and, after a short pause, "You'll say I did too much *D*."

I stared straight into her eyes, noticing the small, telltale tick that always manifested itself on her right eyelid when she had done too much drugs for too long a time. "*She's wired*," I said to myself.

"I *won't* say you did too much *D*," I lied. "What's going on?"

As I continued to stare at Kathy her naturally full and attractive face grew thin and pale before my eyes. The air in the room began to thicken and become more charged. It was becoming difficult for me to catch my breath. The knick-knacks scattered around the room appeared to be revving up like tiny dragsters on a starting line. Ready, at the slightest provocation, to blast off into deep space.

"Well?" I said, persisting in my gaze, despite what was going on around me.

After a lengthy pause Kathy spoke . . .

"I saw a vision," she said quietly. "A visitor . . . from another dimension." She added, her head slightly bowed.

"What?" I remarked, somewhat startled by her claim.

"I *saw* . . . a visitor from another dimension," she said, a little irritated this time.

I slowly nodded my head up and down. "Hmmm," I said – all the while thinking, "*She did do too much D-5*."

"You *saw* a visitor from another dimension," I went on. "And, uh, just *what* did he look like . . . Or was it a *she*?" I added teasingly.

"*Todd is going to enjoy this,*" I mused to myself.

"He . . . looked like a . . . priest," she began, ". . . or maybe a god or something. Somebody holy . . . It's hard for me to describe him," she went on, staring off into space, as if trying to stamp the image of what she had seen back into her mind. Then she continued. "He was tall . . . about six, or maybe even seven feet . . . and he wore a heavy robe that was made of a silver-blue material. He had long white hair and a beard."

I could see that she was struggling to get a more accurate description of what she had seen . . . Or *thought* she had seen.

"Everything around him seemed to be caught up in a whirlwind," she went on, "and bathed in some kind of a . . . green phosphorescence. Long, brown, wings were sticking out from the back of his robe. They hung from his shoulders all the way to the floor . . . Like giant bat's wings. They were . . . fleshy . . . *Ugly*." She concluded, wincing a bit as she spoke.

I know I was acting irrational, now – when I think back – but the more I listened to Kathy describing in detail what she had seen, the more her story began to sound, at least, *marginally* plausible. I hesitated for a moment. "And . . . did he say anything?" I questioned.

"You're not going to believe me".

"I *will* believe you," I now said, a little impatiently, "What did he say."

Two resounding sparks rent the ether. The candles flickered menacingly. The air in the room brushed mysteriously past my face and the howling wind outside caused the windows to rattle abhorrently in their decaying sills. I felt my stomach begin to tighten. Reason told me that what she had experienced was nothing more than a "*D*" induced hallucination. But, something far back in the recesses of my mind – something ancient and more *knowledgeable* than my conscious thoughts – grimly reminded me that in this universe . . . and especially in this room tonight . . . *anything* was possible.

"Well?" I said, still trying to appear cool and collected. But by this time I was beginning to feel far from cool . . . *Or* collected, for that matter.

"His mouth didn't move when he spoke," she continued. "He talked to me through my mind. His head and his eyes moved, but what he said could only be heard inside my head."

"What the *hell* did he say to you!?" I shouted impatiently.

She stared at me for a moment. A bit shocked at my outburst. Then she answered.

"Vazrom. That's what he said . . . Yes . . . Vazrom."

"*Vazrom?*" I asked, a bit puzzled, "What the hell does *Vazrom* mean?" (*That was not the actual word that was spoken. I will not now . . . nor ever, repeat that word again.*)

"It means . . . that the world – the world, as *we* know it – will be no more in four days," she answered, staring straight into my eyes.

I heard a slight clattering sound to my left and looked – just in time to see a small lead soldier slip behind one of the books on the bookshelf.

"It means," she continued, after a slight pause, "that, there is nothing we can do to stop what will happen . . . But, that there *is* something we can do which may allow us both to survive."

The hair on my head had become wet and matted. I could feel tiny, 'electric' beads of sweat forming on my forehead. The aura from the candles suddenly changed their hue, causing the room to appear subterranean and foreboding. Long, baneful shadows suddenly slunk out from nowhere and all the objects in the room began to take on a depraved, unearthly appearance. Grotesque, surreal *Things* began peering out at me from behind bookcases and from the recesses of dark, shrouded corners. "*It's possible,*" I thought to myself, "*Anything is possible.*"

"It means," she continued, the timbre of her voice rising a few decibels, while staring at me with an intently strange look in her eyes, "that, if I follow his instructions . . . we *may* have a chance to survive."

"*May* survive?" I said, taken aback. And then I thought: "*Could all that have been communicated to her in just one word? Of course it could,*" I concluded, remembering the three immutable laws of knowledge: The Known, the Unknown . . . and the Unknowable. "*What did I really <u>know</u> about anything anyway?*" I thought.

I was almost too afraid to ask, but knew that I had to. "What is it you have to do?"

Kathy sat there for a long while, staring straight at me. Droplets of icy liquid began speeding down the groove in my back like tiny soapbox racers competing for best time. The wind again shouldered itself fiercely against the front of the building. I felt the entire structure lurch under the pressure. The whole room began to shift and fluctuate. Everything seemed to be turning into a clear, plastic-like jell . . . The air, the flickering candles . . . Everything. Time itself seemed to cease movement. I could hardly think at all. My mind felt as though it was screeching to a painful, grinding halt. I could feel Kundalini – the *Coiling Serpent*

– trying to force its way up through my intestines. I was being drawn, against my very will, to the *Edge*. That edge; where every Archfiend, known and unknown to the intellect has sway. That unholy, malevolent brink, deep within the cerebellum, where the Monarch of Perdition reigns supreme. That thin lip, deep within the human psyche where, once you slip over it, all conscious control vanishes. And, like in the final panel of Bosch's *'Garden'*, you are plunged, headlong, into the abyss – while all hell *truly* breaks loose around you. A verse from a song by Donovan raced through my head:

"You got to pick up every stitch
The rabbit's runnin' in the ditch . . .
Oh, noooo . . .
Must be the Season of the Witch!"

With great difficulty, I forced my self to speak . . .

"Well . . . What do you have to do?" I said again. This time I spoke in a hoarse whisper. It seemed as if every moment – every *second* – marked by the massive, glass encased time-clock crouching ominously in the corner to my left was drawing me closer and closer into an actual waking nightmare . . . *TICK! . . . TICK! . . . TICK!*

"In order for us to survive," Kathy began, cutting into my grisly thoughts, "I must give away all of our possessions to the poor . . . All, except for one."

"All of our possessions?" I quizzed. " . . . All, except for *one*? . . . The *poor*?" I could actually *feel* the atoms in my brain splitting as they tried to comprehend what she had just said.

"Yes," she affirmed, more calmly now "*All* of our possessions . . . All except for *one* of each thing."

"One of each thing? What the *hell* are you talking about!?" My mind was now a rolling turmoil.

"You know," she said, beginning to explain in more detail, "if we have two shirts, I must give one to the poor; and if we have two spoons, I have to give one to the poor; and if we have . . ."

Kathy then drifted on for some time about what she was supposed to keep and what she was supposed to give to the poor.

My original theory regarding Kathy's mental status slowly began to steal its way back into my head. The more I listened to her, the more convinced I became of the following three factors. One: that she had done *too* much D-5. Two: that she had been up *way* too long. And, three: that she was now *completely* out of it.

"*She's hallucinating!*" I thought to myself, "*She's just . . . hallucinating!*" . . . "*Thank God!*" I added, as a slightly manic burble involuntarily burst from my lips—releasing my internal tension like the safety valve on an over-heated pressure cooker. I had almost been completely taken in by her somewhat believable – but now – after hearing about spoons, shirts and such – completely ludicrous – tale.

Immediately I felt a wave of calmness envelop my being. I looked about the room. It appeared to be wobbling a bit, as if it were stretching itself. Then, after a moment, it relaxed, settled back down, and all seemed to return to normal.

"Kathy," I said, calmer now and trying to maintain my composure, "I know I told you I wouldn't say this, and you're probably not going to believe me right now, but you *did* do too much *D-5,* you've been up too long and you're also hallucinating. You need to lie down and get some sleep."

"That's not true!" she screamed angrily back at me. ". . . Not *true!* I *knew* you were going to say that! I saw him! I *did!*" She crunched herself up into a little ball and began sobbing pitifully.

"Kathy," I said, trying to remain calm, "just *listen* to what you're saying. This 'Visitor' of yours wants you to give away all that we have, except for one of each thing, to the poor. We're jobless, drug-using Hippies. Who is *poorer* than we are! You're just a little spaced, that's all. All you need is a some rest and you'll be fine."

She didn't acknowledge my presence at all . . . She just lay there weeping sorrowfully like a small child.

I stared at her for moment and then got up, walked over to the couch, gently picked her up and carried her to the bedroom. I laid her down on the bed, lit the small candle that sat on the wooden packing crate at the bedside and covered her with a blanket. I then returned to the front room and slowly looked around. Everything seemed to be in order. Everything except for a certain indescribable 'demeanor' that I just couldn't seem to put my finger on – but was there nonetheless – abiding in the room. Finally, finding nothing visible to attribute the odd sensation to, I blew out the candles, walked back to the bedroom and slipped exhaustedly beneath the covers next to Kathy.

I tenderly touched Kathy's body, trying to comfort her. Her body was clammy, cold and rigid as a cadaver. In the dim light of the candle I could see her eyes . . . frozen wide with anxiety. *"I'm going to have some job talking her out of this one,"* I thought.

As I lie next to her stroking her hair I tried to explain the complex activity that goes on inside of a brain that has been deprived of sleep for three days – and inundated every few hours with *D*-5. I told her that the brain *needs* to dream, that it's part of the body's natural function, and that, if you withhold sleep from the body for too long, the brain will begin dreaming while you're awake . . . I also reminded her of how "unpredictable" Todd told us that *D*-5 might turn out to be.

"Don't worry, Kat," I said, trying hard to be reassuring – *I had also experienced a number of near-similar episodes myself* – "All you need is some sleep and you'll be fine."

She slowly turned as if in a trance and looked up at me. But I could see by her glassy stare that only *part* of her had been listening. The other part was listening for the return of the *Visitor* in the front room.

IN SPITE OF her condition, Kathy finally fell into a deep sleep. As I looked down at her it seemed as though, while in this deep state of repose, all of her fear and stress was slowly being drawn away. Before my eyes she began transforming back into the beautiful girl-woman that I had first met two years ago on 2nd Avenue and St. Marks Place. I smiled and said, softly, "All you need is one good night's sleep, and you'll be just like new again. I promise."

However, that was not to be. For when Kathy awoke late the next afternoon, her condition remained much the same as it had been the night before . . . If not slightly worsened. She forbade me turn on any of the lights in the apartment. Except for the small candle burning by the bedside, the entire apartment was to be kept dark. She also refused to eat or leave the bedroom. She just lie there, looking toward the front room . . . Waiting for the *Visitor* to return. I knew she was still 'spaced', but no matter what I said to try to convince her that it was all just a bad fantasy, it wouldn't sink in.

Another strange thing I experienced was that, although I *knew* all this was just the side effects of *D-5*, I just couldn't bring myself to enter the front room any more. Every time that I even passed *near* it, I experienced a cold vibration – something foreign and unloving – emanating from behind the curtain.

By the second day the situation with Kathy began to grow even worse. She would neither eat, sleep, nor even speak now. She would occasionally sip a cup of tea, but only with much prodding and cajoling on my part.

By the third day I was nearly at my wit's end. Walking through the apartment was like feeling my way through a dark, shadowy labyrinth in a cheap horror film. Every time I left the house for something – cigarettes mostly – I would return to the same dismal scene: No lights – except for the small candle burning endlessly at the bedside – no radio . . . No nothing. Nothing except Kathy . . . lying in bed, covers pulled tightly up to her chin, staring out into the front room with eyes as big as silver dollars.

On the fourth day I could no longer endure being in the house and, in spite of the extreme cold, left for a long walk down along the East River to gather my thoughts.

"I *have* to figure something out," I said angrily, as I walked faster to keep warm, ". . . Some way out of this . . . *insanity!* I can't take this madness anymore!"

I reached the East River and was leaning over the rail, staring at the raw sewage drifting out to sea, all the while racking my mind for a solution to this mess – when it hit me.

"I've got it!" I cried out loud. I turned and quickly began walking back to the apartment.

Kathy believed that, in order for us to be saved she must " . . . give everything away – *except for one of each: . . . one spoon, one shirt,*" et cetera – to the poor. Fine. If that was true for her, then it must also be true for other people. All *anyone* had to do to be saved was give away all – except for one – of his or her belongings, right? Well, then shouldn't they be given the same opportunity as we were? "Yes!" I said. *"Yes! I've got it!"*

My plan, once I got home, was to tell Kathy that I was going to take her to the Daily News and the New York Times so that she could tell them all that she had seen and heard from this '*Visitor*' of hers. The papers could then print it up and everyone that read the story would also have a chance to be saved. The hope was that once confronted with such a realistic, down-to-earth, scenario, she would see the foolishness of her thinking, snap out of her delusion, and, once again, return to her normal self. *"That's it!"* I cried, walking faster now. "That'll pull her out of it!"

I couldn't wait to get home. I was so thrilled with my idea that when I arrived at our building I began calling her name while still in the hallway. "Kathy! . . . *Kathy!* Listen!

I got a great idea!" I hollered, digging in my pocket for the keys. "We're going to go to the newspapers and tell them everything! Come on, Kat, *get up!*" I fumbled with my key, finally unlocking the door and flinging it open wide. "Kathy! . . . Come on, *Get up!*" I called again, running into the bedroom, foolishly tripping in the dark over the Police-lock bar that was still wedged firmly into the kitchen floor.

The bedroom was dark and there was absolutely no sound. The candle that had been burning by the side of the bed was out. I switched on the small lamp that was attached to the head of the bed and pulled back the blanket. Kathy was not in bed. Still keyed up over my plan, I shambled through the dark, into the bathroom and then the kitchen looking for her – switching on lights as I went. I thought that maybe, while I was away, she had finally come to her senses and had gotten up to eat or something.

No Kathy.

I paused for a moment trying to organize my thoughts. And then, in a flash it came to me. "The front room!" I said out loud. I quickly turned around and faced the curtains. I hesitated for just a moment, recalling the weird sensation I had experienced as I passed near them a few days ago. But then, thinking that it was all just part of the *"Mále Fantasía",* I seized the curtains, frantically jerked them aside, and rushed into the front room.

The room was exactly the same as it had been four days ago . . . Except for the following: In the center of the room, among the clutter, a small black candle was burning. There was also a strong, concentrated presence of ozone hanging in the air.

I looked about. Kathy was not there. I ran out of the

apartment and into the street – racing from door to door, inquiring if anyone had seen her . . . No one had.

I rushed over to Todd's place two blocks away, distraughtly relaying to him all that had happened. He was silent for a moment, appearing to be staring at something on the desk in front of him. Then he said, with total disregard to what I had told him about Kathy's disappearance: "Something must have gone wrong during the preparation of the last batch of elixir."

I finally lost control. "*Fuck* all of that shit, Todd!" I screamed. "*Where* is Kathy!?"

He dismissed my outburst with a wave of his hand, and then calmly went on to say that he must have missed one of the procedures. "Or maybe," he claimed, he had "mixed the chemicals incorrectly." He said that he had written down everything that he had done that day. He said that he would go over everything again and find out what went wrong. "Don't worry, " he said, absentmindedly pushing through the litter of papers on his desk, "I'll get it right this time." Then he turned and walked off into another room, mumbling to himself, as if I had never been there.

I stared after him in total disbelief. In his urgency to create a drug that would be everyone's "Ticket to Heaven", Todd had become totally detached from the reality around him – and, more important, to what appeared to have happened to Kathy. I just stood and stared for another moment at the litter, the stained, glass tubes and laboratory beakers, and crumpled papers strewn all about the apartment, then shook my head and walked out the door into the freezing cold.

The next morning I abandoned my apartment taking only two knapsacks with me. One filled with books and other with clothes. I never returned.

THIRTY YEARS HAVE past since the night that Kathy claimed to have seen the Visitor and the inexplicable incident that took place four days later. I cannot attest to the validity of what I think I remember. That is the most frustrating factor of this account that I must deal with. Was there a *real* visitation? Or, was what Kathy said she saw just the consequences of a bad batch of D-5? Did Kathy really disappear? Or did she just run off while I was gone, leaving me, her friends and all her belongings behind. Did it all really happen the way I *now* perceive it? I have tried, but have never succeeded, to my satisfaction, in sorting out the circumstances leading up to, and following, those baffling events. What, in fact actually did occur on that specific night, and four days later, will remain a mystery to me until the end of my days. I know only this: . . . That neither I, nor anyone that I know, has seen or heard from Kathy since.

I have kept in touch with Todd's whereabouts through the years, and still correspond with him occasionally. He is confined in a psychiatric hospital in Maine. I send him legal pads, pencils, and other small necessities that he requests when he writes me. He is editing and correcting, from memory, the errors that he feels he made when he copied the old monk's original manuscripts. He is also working on a new, more stable – and more potent – formula for the elixir. He will call it D-6.

THE UNDERCOVER
AGENT

"Open up the window, let some air into dis room
I think I'm almost chokin' from the smell of stale
perfume . . .

The radio is blastin' someone's knockin' at the door
I seen so many things, I don't wanna see no more . . ."
- 3 Dog Night
"Mama Told Me Not To Come"

The place: Southern Florida. The time: the Dawning of the Age of Aquarius. The season: the Endless Summer. It was the Era of the Hippie. Flower Power. Long hair. Drugs. Sex. Rock n Roll. Peace. Love. No bras. It was all cool, man...

ME AND TOMMY were cruising across the MacArthur Causeway on my newly purchased Capriola. It was an Italian café racer. I got it at a repo auction for two hundred bucks. It was fire engine red and trimmed with white pin striping. At one time, it was used strictly for racing but had been slightly modified to be street legal: Somebody put a headlight on it. I could feel the deep thrumming of the dual exhausts on my legs as I dropped it into fourth gear.

It felt cool, man. I dug it.

It was a perfect Saturday night. Warm – but not too warm. Just enough breeze. The night sky was cloudless. The stars sparkled and glinted like tiny diamonds set in a big, black, velvet-lined box. "Yeah," I think to myself as I glance up, "Another Saturday night in Paradise."

But, unlike the weather in Florida, who could've predicted the uncanny events that were about to unfold.

THE REASON THAT Tommy and me were driving to the Beach – Miami Beach, that is – this particular night was that he wanted to introduce me to some people he had met a few days ago through his wife, Judy. According to him, they were "a little weird, but very cool."

At the time, Tommy, Judy and me all were living in the same semi-seedy motel in Southwest Miami. The place wasn't too bad. It had air conditioning – that worked most of the time – a fridge, a stove and TV. The only drag was the furniture. It was that Norwegian-styled stuff; done up in Aqua, and Pumpkin-colored, Naugahyde. Uncool colors, to say the least – and also, very sticky when the AC cashes in.

Tommy and me had, somehow, passed ourselves off as 'handymen' to the owner, so we never had to pay any rent. We'd move a few air conditioners, change some faucet washers, do a little painting, clean up a little around the place, and that was it. A very groovy arrangement . . . being that neither of us had a steady job . . . But, that's another story.

I SPED ACROSS the causeway, wheeled left off the exit

ramp and headed up Collins Avenue. Then I drove up the coast – passing all the big hotels on the way – until I felt Tommy tap me on my shoulder. I turned and saw him pointing to a small cottage a short way from the main road and over to our right. I cut off Collins Avenue, drove down a winding, sandy road and, after a few hundred feet, arrived at the house.

It was a small, Caribbean-styled cottage, painted in traditional Floridian-Pink-and-Turquoise. The house was surrounded by a few Palmetto trees that kept it more or less hidden from the main road. The entrance faced the beach. I pulled alongside one of the Palmetto trees, cut the engine and kicked down the stand. Tommy and me got off and walked up the sandy path that led to the entrance of the pad. We reached the door, hesitated a moment, and then proceeded to announce our presence.

There was no doorbell. After a small search, I discovered a long, heavy, silver chain, which hung from a bracket next to the door. When I pulled it, what sounded like, five or six metal, wind chimes, began jangling all at once. From inside the house the mesmerizing drone of sitar music drifted forth.

Slowly – very slowly – the jalousie windows on the door began to creak open. The thick, pungent odor of incense wafted out and hung gelatinously in the air. Suddenly, at one of the open slats, slowly emerging from the murky twilight deep within, a pair of lavender-tinted-kaleidoscopic-fly-eyed-psychedelic-sunglasses appear.

Me and Tommy look at each other, shrug, and then turn back to the lavender-tinted-kaleidoscopic-fly-eyed-psychedelic-sunglasses peering at us, and wait.

Eventually the door squeezes open – coming to an abrupt halt when it reaches the end of a thick, four-inch security chain – and this strange cat pops his head out. He stares at me and Tommy for almost a full minute, giving us this weird, bewildered look. Then, after flipping up one lens – just one – of his lavender-tinted-kaleidoscopic-fly-eyed-psychedelic-sunglasses, the cat breaks into a big, fat grin and says, "Hey, Tommy! Wow! Like Wow! Come on in, man!" He unhooks the chain, opens the door, and we step into the usual 'Psychedelica' that was the vogue at the time . . .

CANDLES OF EVERY color, size and shape burned everywhere. Over time, the melting wax had dripped and coagulated into thick, multicolored stalagmites that drooped surrealistically over the sides of all the tables. All about the room, numerous varieties of incense burners were spewing out their thick, smudgy perfumes. Big, fat Buddhas issued rivulets of myrrh from round trays on their mammoth bellies. Diabolical brass skulls disgorged thick clouds of unidentifiable yellowish vapors from their vacuous eye sockets. Youthful porcelain fairy-nymphs with exquisite Lilliputian breasts, positioned on tiptoe, bore silver vessels of steaming frankincense.

The entire floor of the living room was covered with Indian rugs. What appeared to be hundreds of paisley pillows were chucked helter-skelter all about. A large couch upholstered entirely in hand-dyed Indian block-print squatted low and heavy near the center the room. A coffee table sat in front of the couch. It was large, square, and also very low—about twelve inches from the floor—and bore all manner of mind titillating paraphernalia. Tiny pewter statues of Gandalf the Magician, and other characters from Tolkien's '*Ring* trilogy, idly lounged about on the coarse, uneven surface. Intricately hand woven wicker baskets were placed here and there – filled to their brim with wooden, Norwegian hand-painted, and highly polished alabaster, eggs. Three or four black and red lacquered Chinese magic puzzle-boxes also sat on the table.

The walls and ceiling of the pad had all been sprayed with a flat, black primer. Aside from the huge array of sputtering candles, there were no noticeable electric lamps or lighting fixtures. The only electric lighting that I noticed came from the black-lights hanging from tracks on the ceiling. These were concentrated on the walls and used to illuminate the bizarre day-glow paintings portrayed there. An immense two-headed, multicolored parrot stared vacantly out from unknown regions deep within one darkened wall. Erotic reproductions gleaned from the Kama Sutra swirled mystically through the shadowy ether. Fuchsia and Chartreuse peace signs were painted here and there.

This pad was very cool, indeed, man.

As I stared at this psychedelic vista, I began to experience a strange sensation. It was almost as if I was slowly being transported into a live rendition of a Peter Max poster – or maybe transcendentally thrust into the temple scene from Aldous Huxley's "*Island*". I couldn't figure out just which. I glanced over at Tommy to see if he was in the same state of mind that I was. He appeared to be unmoved by the surroundings.

I then turned my eyes from the otherworldly scenes depicted on the walls and again looked down at the large coffee table. Upon closer examination, I noticed five or six different length roach clips – along with ten or fifteen packs of rolling papers – each boasting a distinct and unique flavor and color – strewn about among the clutter. Also on the table – and in the very center of this, somewhat fanciful setting – sat a massive wooden bowl filled with Boo. You know . . . *Boo*. Herb. Grass. Maryjane. Reefer. Pot. Weed . . . Cannabis Sa-*ti*-va, man.

"Wow. *This pad is really cool*," I think to myself again, while taking in the whole scene and smiling, "*I dig it*."

While still thinking of how cool the pad was, I hear someone say, "Like, Wow. So you're Tommy's friend." I turn and look up. "I'm Tamarind (I think that's what he called himself - or something like that, anyway)," the guy who opened the door for us is saying, while standing right in front of me – smiling like some Chinese waiter who is waiting for me to order "Slimp, Fly Lice", or something.

"Hey," I say, trying not to appear rude.

Besides the lavender-tinted-kaleidoscopic-fly-eyed-psychedelic-sunglasses, which give him the weird appearance of having big insect-eyes, he's wearing a faded purple tee shirt with a picture of R. Crumb's famous "Keep on Truckin' " scene painted on it. He's also wearing the traditional, faded, cut-off jeans. His hair is dirty-blond – Dirty – Blond – and droops limply down around his lanky shoulders. His beard is long, untrimmed and scrawny. Even in the rich glow from the candles, his face appears pale. As I stare at him, I wonder how long it has been since he has been outdoors.

"Peace, man," He says while giving me the peace sign.

"Peace," I reply, shooting him the peace sign back.

"Wow, man. Wow. Like, sit down, man," he says, dreamily stroking his scraggly beard. I look over at Tommy. He looks back, shrugs and casually sits down on one of the large, paisley pillows lying by the coffee table. I shrug back at him and do the same.

Then the cat turns and shouts, "Hey Tippy! (I think that's what he called his old lady - or something like that, anyway.) Wow, like, look who's here! Wow!"

Tippy was in – what I later found out to be – the kitchen. It was separated from the living room by a long curtain made from strings of big, brown, wooden beads. There seemed to be an indistinct scuffing or "clacking" sound coming from behind the curtain.

When Tippy failed to appear, Tamarind raised his hands and hollered: "Hey, Tip, Come on, man! Come on out an' say hello to Tommy and his friend."

"Be right there, Tam," a light cheerful voice answered from beyond the beads. The unidentifiable "clacking" sound ceased. Then, suddenly, with a colossal WHOOSH! WHOOSH! WHOOSH! the big, brown, wooden beads thrash wildly together, separate and . . . Viola! . . . Tippy!

As far as I could see, Tippy was clothed only in a sky-blue, wash-worn chambray shirt – Triple X, Large would be my off-the-cuff measurement. The sleeves, although rolled up many times, came to rest just a few inches below her petite elbows. Thirteen or fourteen strands of love beads dangled freely about her neck – all of contrasting size, design and shape.

Oh, yeah. I almost forgot. She also had on a pair of

those lavender-tinted-kaleidoscopic-fly-eyed-psychedelic-sunglasses . . . Except that hers were tinted a deep blood red.

"Wow. Like, hi," she cooed lightly . . . "Wow, I'm stoned," she also added.

"C'mon dudes," says Tamarind, picking up the enormous wooden bowl from the table and shoving it in our faces, "Like, try some of this stuff. It's out of sight, man. I got it from a Jamaican dude last week . . . It's straight from the island, man."

"Cool," I say agreeably – while wondering just what island he was talking about – "Let's check it out."

Tamarind leans over and hands Tippy the bowl. She sets it down in front of her, rolls up her huge shirtsleeves, pulls four sheets of rolling paper from a pack of Easy Wider – Banana Flavor – and proceeds to roll four very large torpedoes. When she finishes, she hands Tamarind – then both me and Tommy – a 'bone'. Tommy and me smile thanks, sneak a gleeful look at each other, and grab for an idle candle to light up.

But, just as we were about to fire up, someone knocks on the door. Tamarind answers it and then hollers, "Hey Tommy. Like, it's your wife, man." Tommy gets up and goes to the door. Him and Judy are there whispering for a minute. Then Tommy turns around and says to me: "Listen, man, gotta go. I'll be back in a little while, okay?

In a second the door slams and Tommy is gone.

It's just me, now. Sitting here with two cats that I only met five minutes ago. I'm beginning to feel a little bit uneasy.

Tamarind looks at me and says: "Cm'on, man, light up.

The shit is really outta sight. You're gonna dig it, man."

Now, don't get me wrong. I like to smoke dope. I love to smoke dope. I just don't dig smoking it with strangers. Makes me paranoid. However, not wanting to look like some kind of a 'drool', I say again, "Sure, man, lets check it out." We all grab a candle and light up – All the while I'm thinking to myself, "I hope this scene stays cool, man."

APPROXIMATELY TEN MINUTES later, everything around me starts slowing down. Like, everything is moving in slow motion. And ten minutes after that – I say ten minutes . . . but I can't, in reality, tell you how long it actually was – between Shankar on the sitar, the incense, the black-lights and the lavender-tinted-kaleidoscopic-fly-eyed-psychedelic-sunglasses – which, for some strange reason, are now sitting on the bridge of my nose – I couldn't have told you if I had died and gone to Nirvana, been transported into the last panel of Bosch's Garden of Earthly Delights . . . or had just plain ol' peed in my traditional, faded, cut-off jeans.

I look around and, by what I am seeing, quickly dig that I'm totally wasted out of my mind – For I am no longer sitting in the living room. I am now sitting in, what appears to be, some bizarre, subterranean dining hall, inhabited by two deranged Hippies who are staring at me like I'm about to be the next burnt offering to their, fiendish, demented – and very hungry – god.

I stare rigidly back. I'm getting paranoid now. I can feel it. The pressure is building in my spine. I try to fight the feeling off but it won't go away. "This scene is becoming uncool," I say to myself – starting not to dig what's going on. If I could've stood up by myself and found the door – without falling flat on my puss, that is – I would've split out of there "Mucho Pronto" . . . But, unfortunately, I was in La-La Land – Big Time.

Bummer, man.

I hear a strange sound and look up. Multiple Tippys are standing in front of me – all saying what sounds like, "Oh-bla-dee, Oh-bla-daa, Quirk, Oh Tine . . . Ye?" Or something weird like that. I stare back at them – stiff as a catatonic.

Shankar is wailing a mean solo on his ax.

Finally, I shake my head, take off the lavender-tinted-kaleidoscopic-fly-eyed-psychedelic-sunglasses – the multiple Tippys quiver and merge into one – and, with much effort, manage to pronounce, "Wha?"

As I force myself to listen more closely, her words begin to unjumble themselves and I hear her saying, "Come into the kitchen, man. I want to show you something . . . okay?"

I get up like one afflicted with acute vertigo, take her hand, and follow her as best as I can across the dimly lit and incense-ladened chamber. And, with a stupendous WHOOSH! WHOOSH! WHOOSH! from the big, brown, wooden-beaded curtain, we arrive in the kitchen.

THERE'S NOT MUCH to see. Just some dirty dishes and half-full glasses sitting in the sink. Tippy points to a table over by the wall. I turn and look. There, sitting on the table – along with a box of kitchen matches and a pack of Zig Zag – is an enormous wooden bowl – identical to the one in the parlor – filled almost to the brim with Boo.

Tippy picks up what looks like, a large wooden scraper out of the sink. She hands it to me, points at the bowl on the table and says, "Here, man. Wanna scrape some of the seeds outa this stuff?"

I'm so smashed I can't really dig what she's saying – so I just stand there gawking at her with a big, stupid, half-grin plastered on my face.

"Here," she says again. Whereupon she sits me down at the table, puts the scraper in my hand, my hand in the bowl, and commences to vigorously stir the grass around saying, "See? Like this, okay?" Then she turns and splits out of the room – WHOOSH! WHOOSH! WHOOSH!

With the scraper in the bowl, I start running my hand round and round – Scuff . . . Clack-Clack. Scuff . . . Clack-Clack – realizing now what the clacking and scuffing sound was that I had heard before.

I feel like I'm in the kitchen for hours. Of course, at this point there was no way of computing time. I also felt like I was coming down and had rolled myself a joint from the boo in the bowl.

Like, big mistake, man.

The sound of the scraper against the inside of the bowl now has me spellbound. I'm really starting to get into it. From the other side of the curtain I can hear Steppenwolf breaking into "Magic Carpet Ride". It seems to have a calming effect on my nerves.

Like, Very cool, man, I think to myself, Very cool, indeed.

In my mind, I'm now sailing through the heavens on my own private magic carpet – which is being steered by the way I'm moving the scraper in the bowl of boo – when, all of a sudden, I hear this tremendous WHOOSH! WHOOSH! WHOOSH! And, as if hit by a bolt of lightning, I'm hurled back into the world again. I look up from the bowl and there, standing in front of me is Tippy . . . But it's not the same Tippy as before. No, it's not the same sweet little Tippy that had walked out of this room an hour or so ago. This Tippy is a mean Tippy . . . A sinister Tippy . . . A Tippy that seems to have some ominous, foreboding . . . something . . . going on in the back of her mind . . . This was a bad little Tippy.

She stares at me with a malicious looking smirk on her pinched, little face and says, "Hey, man. Come on out into the parlor . . . Someone . . . wants to meet you."

The sound of her voice seems to change every vibration in the air into something evil and pernicious.

"Whoa," I think to myself. "Bummer, man."

"Come on!" she shouts.

I slowly get up from the table thinking, *"Oh, Christ, man! Like, what now!"*

She takes me by the hand, we both WHOOSH! WHOOSH! WHOOSH! through the big, brown, wooden beads and, in a flash, we are standing in, what was once, just a simple subterranean dinning hall – but is now the horrifying Temple of Kali: The Gruesome Goddess of Death.

I hear an unintelligible sound and turn to see what it is. It's Tamarind. He's standing off in the shadows, ominously pointing a bony finger at a dim figure sitting on the couch across the room.

I stare hard to where he is pointing. Through the smoky nebula of incense, the black lights, and the dim flicker of candles, I observe a dark shadow sitting on the couch. I can't really make out who it is so I try to stagger a little closer. I'm having a hard time walking. I look down. The temple floor seems to have turned into something resembling sticky, soggy oatmeal. While slowly squishing through the sticky sludge in extra slo-mo, I hear, what sounds like, a pint-sized tittering coming from Tippy's direction: "Tee, Hee-Hee-Hee . . . Tee, Hee-Hee-Hee . . . Tee, Hee-Hee-Hee."

"Uncool, man," I'm thinking. " . . . Very uncool."

"That's Mike," I hear Tamarind say. And then, after what seems like an extra long pause, he continues: ". . . .He wants to . . . Meet . . . you."

I glance over at Tamarind and notice that he is smiling somewhat perversely. On the stereo, the Chambers Brothers are singing "The Time Has Come Today".

I turn and slosh up to the guy so I can get a better look at him.

"Hold up a minute!" I say to myself as I draw nearer, "This dude is lookin' like VERY weird."

I lean over a little closer and. . . ."Yo! Wait a minute!" I say again to myself. "This dude is wearin' a mask!" . . . And, sure enough, he was! He was wearing one of those Groucho Marx things! You know . . . the thick black horned-rimmed glasses, the dark, furry eyebrows, and the big hooked nose with the huge, square mustache hanging below it.

Things are now exceedingly uncool – And I'm not digging the scene at all.

I turn towards Tippy and Tamarind—all the while thinking to myself: " . . . *That CAN'T be their real names . .*

.", and finally stammer, "What's . . . goin' on, man!"

No response.

I think: "*Did I just say that . . . Or, did I just think it?*"

In the background, I hear the group, WAR: "*I was slippin' into darkness . . . When I herrrd my motha say . . . whashesay, whashesay, whashesay . . .*"

The dude is sitting there with his hand stretched out in my direction. "Hi-ya, man," he says to me.

I'm too confused at this point to answer. "Like, who is this guy?" I'm thinking. I stare deep into his mug. Deep . . . Deep, beyond that stupid mask . . . Deep . . . Deep . . . Deeper!

Suddenly my mind reels. "Sonofabitch!" I squeak. "It's Nicky Nazaretti! Nicky the Narc! It's fuckin' Nicky the Narc!"

I whirl around and glare straight at Tippy and Tamarind – if that's what they're really called – seeking an explanation. "Yo, man. Like what the fuck's goin' on, man!"

Blank stares.

(WAR again) " . . . *You been slippin' into darkness . . . Pretty sooooon . . . you gonna pay! . . . Yeeaahh!*"

All of a sudden, it becomes alarming clear to me. These two cats – Tamarind and Tippy – or Tippy and Tamarind – whatever – have just set me up! Yeah! . . . Set me up to get busted with all that shit they had me sifting out there in the kitchen! And busted by none other than Nicky the Narc! Nicky the fucking Narc! . . . who, only last week in Miami, told me – in no fewer words – how much he hated us "fuckin' longhairs." . . . and had personally promised to bury my "Hippie ass" the first chance that he got.

I couldn't believe it! I was gonna get popped and go to jail . . . Tonight too! I vaguely wondered if Tommy – my so-called friend – didn't also have some hand in this whole thing.

I begin to envision myself being booked down at the Dade County Jail. And then being taken – screaming and kicking – up to the eighteen-man cells . . . Stoned out of my mind. The horror of it all suddenly strikes me with the force of a Mack truck. "There's no way I'm goin' to jail tonight!" I think to myself, in a sudden fit of cold-blooded terror. " . . . Not like this, man!"

Fighting off a sudden urge to bolt for the door – knowing full well that I was so blitzed that I would probably trip over my own two feet and fall smack on my puss into the oatmeal – and excepting the fact that the 'party' was over – I pull myself together as best as I can, and look straight at Nicky. He's still holding out his hand and staring at me with, what appears to be, a half-witted grin on his face. The longer I look, the more distinctly I can see Nicky grinning – sneering – at me from behind that stupid mask. I can see his tiny, red, porker-like eyes peering out from behind those thick, moronic frames. I can even see that little pug nose of his, hiding behind that asinine, hooked, plastic thing he was wearing.

"What a fuckin' pack of morons!" I say to myself, turning from Nicky and looking straight at Tippy and Tamarind – if those are their real names. "They must think that I can't dig what's going on here! 'Oh, yeah, I'm stoned, alright. But stoned don't mean stupid! An' what's Nicky supposed to be . . . Some kind of undercover agent, or something? Christ, man! Like what a set of Ka-honies!"

Again, I turn and look hard at Nicky. He is still staring at me . . . Holding out his hand, smiling, and saying, "Hey, dude, what's wrong?"

I stare right back into his stupid looking kisser and, throwing all abandon to the wind, say, "Hey dude, what's wrong?" mocking his voice as best I can. "Hey dude . . . what's WRONG!? The fucking game is over, man! That's what's wrong . . . Nicky! You can take that stupid shit off, now. I'm hip to you, man!"

"What?" he answers, with an innocent look.

"Yeah . . . *Right*!" is my comeback.

"Like I'm *hip* to you, Nicky!" I continue, "I *pinned* you. I *dug* you, okay? So you can take that stupid lookin' shit off your face now!"

He looks at me quizzically and then says, "What, these?" And with that, he pulls off the thick, dark-rimmed glasses. But the eyebrows, nose, and mustache still remain on his face.

I stare at his mug for a long time. A real long time. Then, turning and looking around at Tippy and Tamarind, I shout, "Like, can somebody tell me just what the hell's goin' on here, man?"

Total silence . . . Except for Jim Morrison's voice over the stereo: "People are strange when you're a stranger . . ."

I turn back to Nicky, slosh right up to him, bend down over him and, reaching for the large, hooked, nose say, "Yeah, and you can take this off too, man, while you're at it!"

With this said, I grab the big hooked nose, tweak it

hard – real hard – and attempt to pull it off, and . . . But it doesn't budge. No, it doesn't budge. Because it's his. Yes. The large, hooked nose, those thick, furry eyebrows – even that stupid mustache . . . Like, they're all his, man.

I'M STANDING IN the middle of the room now, with everyone gawking at me like I'm the original Fiji Mermaid, when all of a sudden the whole scene comes rushing back into focus – well, almost back in focus – the floor is still coated with sticky oatmeal.

"Like, wow, man," I say to myself, while staring around at everybody, "Like, did I just play the misguided fool tonight, or what, man?"

"This guy ain't Nicky the Narc," I say to myself, looking at the guy sitting in front of me – who is now tenderly fingering a large red bruise on the tip of his nose. I turn and look over at the two cats staring at me from across the room. I see that Tippy . . . is just plain ol' Tippy. And Tamarind . . . just plain ol' Tamarind

Shooting for my most 'Hip' stance, and without saying a word to anyone – and silently praying that no one says a word to me either – I very casually turn, slosh over to the door, open it and – swiftly and silently – vanish, like a shadow in the night.

≈ ≈ ≈

It's drizzling outside. I can hear the ocean bubbling and gurgling against the shore. The strong smell of sea-brine fills my nose. I stand with my head turned toward the heavens, letting the cool drops fall on my face. I remain fixed in this position – patiently waiting for the soggy oatmeal under my feet to go away.

Finally, the oatmeal – or whatever it is – dries up, and I achieve touchdown.

Wow, man. Like, what a trip!

I turn, hop on my bike and crank it over. It springs to life with a bursting crack. I gun the engine a few times, kick the stand back, drop it into first gear, pull out onto Collins Avenue and head back to Southwest Miami and my snug little pad.

While I'm cruising back home I idly wonder if there is still any Swiss cheese left in the fridge.

That'd be cool, man. Yeah . . . Very cool, indeed.

Thank you for reading.
Please review this book. Reviews help others find
Absolutely Amazing eBooks and inspire us to keep
providing these marvelous tales.

If you would like to be put on our email list to receive
updates on new releases, contests, and promotions, please
go to AbsolutelyAmazingEbooks.com and sign up.

About the Author

George Cook (G. J. Cook) lives in Key West, Florida. He is originally from Newark, New Jersey. Besides writing short stories, he also writes songs, poetry, and is a blues musician. He was inducted into the Blues Hall of Fame in 2012. At one time he also hand-designed personal greeting cards. He is now semi-retired, occasionally performing blues at venues in the Florida Keys. He has four adult children.

The New
Atlantian Library

NewAtlantianLibrary.com
or AbsolutelyAmazingeBooks.com
or AA-eBooks.com